William F. Tucker, Town Council of Charlestown

Historical Sketch of the Town of Charlestown in Rhode Island

from 1636 to 1876 - Vol. 1

William F. Tucker, Town Council of Charlestown

Historical Sketch of the Town of Charlestown in Rhode Island
from 1636 to 1876 - Vol. 1

ISBN/EAN: 9783337378868

Printed in Europe, USA, Canada, Australia, Japan

Cover: Foto ©Andreas Hilbeck / pixelio.de

More available books at **www.hansebooks.com**

HISTORICAL SKETCH

OF THE

TOWN OF CHARLESTOWN,

IN

RHODE ISLAND,

FROM

1636 TO 1876.

———◆—◆—◆———

TRANSCRIBED AND WRITTEN

BY WILLIAM FRANKLIN TUCKER,

SUPERINTENDENT OF PUBLIC SCHOOLS.

———◆—◆—◆———

BY ORDER OF THE TOWN COUNCIL.

———◆—◆—◆———

G. B. & J. H. UTTER, STEAM PRINTERS, WESTERLY, R. I.
1877.

PRESIDENT'S PROCLAMATION.

BY THE PRESIDENT OF THE UNITED STATES,

A PROCLAMATION.

Whereas, A joint resolution of the Senate and House of Representatives of the United States was duly approved on the 13th day of March last, which resolution is as follows:

" Be it resolved, by the Senate and House of Representatives of the United States of America, in Congress assembled, that it be and is hereby recommended by the Senate and the House of Representatives, to the people of the several States, that they assemble in their several counties or towns on the approaching centennial anniversary of our national independence, and that they cause to have delivered on such day an historical sketch of said county or town from its formation, and that a copy of said sketch may be filed, in print or manuscript, in the Clerk's office of said County, and an additional copy, in print or manuscript, be filed in the office of the Librarian of Congress, to the intent that a complete record may thus be obtained of the progress of our institutions during the first centennial of their existence " ; and

Whereas, It is deemed proper that such recommendation be brought to the notice and knowledge of the people of the United States ;

Now, therefore, I, Ulysses S. Grant, President of the United States, do hereby declare and make known the same, in the hope that the object of such resolution may meet the approval of the people of the United States, and that proper steps may be taken to carry the same into effect.

Given under my hand, at the city of Washington, the 25th day of May, in the year of our Lord 1876, and of the independence of the United States the one hundredth.   U. S. GRANT.

By the President,

HAMILTON FISH, *Secretary of State.*

STATE OF RHODE ISLAND, &c.

IN GENERAL ASSEMBLY, JANUARY SESSION, A. D. 1876.

JOINT RESOLUTION

ON THE

CELEBRATION OF THE CENTENNIAL IN THE SEVERAL CITIES AND TOWNS.

Resolved, the House of Representatives concurring therein, That in accordance with the recommendation of the National Congress, the Governor be requested to invite the people of the several towns and cities of the State, to assemble in their several localities on the approaching Centennial Anniversary of our National Independence, and cause to have delivered on that day an historical sketch of said town or city from its formation, and to have one copy of said sketch, in print or in manuscript, filed in the Clerk's office of said town or city, one copy in the office of the Secretary of State, and one copy in the office of the Librarian of Congress, to the intent that a complete record may thus be obtained of the progress of our institutions during the First Centennial of their existence; and that the Governor be requested to communicate this invitation forthwith to the several towns and city councils in the State.

I certify the foregoing to be a true copy of a resolution passed by the General Assembly of the State aforesaid, on the 20th day of April, A. D. 1876.

{L. s.}   Witness my hand and seal of the State, this 27th day of April, A. D. 1876.

         JOSHUA M. ADDEMAN, *Secretary of State.*

STATE OF RHODE ISLAND.

EXECUTIVE DEPARTMENT, }
PROVIDENCE, April 27th, 1876. }

To the Honorable Town Council of the Town of Charlestown :

Gentlemen : I have the honor herewith to enclose a duly certi-
fied copy of a resolution passed by the General Assembly at its re-
cent session, requesting me to invite the people of the several
towns and cities of the State to assemble in their several localities
on the approaching Centennial Anniversary of our National Independence, and cause to have delivered on such day an historical
sketch of said town or city from its formation.

By pursuing the course suggested by the Resolution of the General Assembly, the people of the State will derive an amount of information which will be invaluable to the present generation, as
showing the wonderful progress of the several towns and cities
since their foundation. It will also be of great value to future generations, when the materials for such sketches now accessible will
have been lost or destroyed by accident, or become more or less
effaced and illegible from time.

Therefore, in pursuance of the request of the General Assembly,
I respectfully and earnestly, through you, invite the people of your
town to carry out the contemplated celebration on the 4th day of
July next.　　　　　　　　HENRY LIPPITT, *Governor.*

PREFACE.

In transcribing and preparing this sketch for publication, the original orthography has been closely followed where it relates to the Colonial Records. The most important facts relative to the settlements which were first made in this colony, and subsequently in this town, I have endeavored to present in a clear and comprehensive manner. From books, newspapers and manuscripts, I have copied to a large extent. Of course, in many instances I have had to peruse a great many books, papers and pamphlets, to gain a little information. No person who has not undertaken to gather such statistical items, can fully comprehend the vast amount of time and labor which are needful to collect them, and to ascertain their connection with previous affairs and establishments. The Records of the proceedings of the General Assembly, as far as they relate to the Niantic or Narragansett Indians, have been copied for this volume.

It is right and just, therefore, to acknowledge my indebtedness to the Rhode Island Colonial Records, to Elisha R. Potter's Early History of Narragansett, to Wilkins Updike's History of the Churches of Rhode Island, and to the Town Records. I must, however, acknowledge my special indebtedness to Charles Cross, Esq., Town Clerk, for his valuable aid in examining the old records, which date back nearly one hundred and forty years; to David Smith, Esq., Superintendent of Public Schools of Westerly, for his generous assistance; and to James N. Kenyon and wife, as well as others whom I have not time to mention.

In proper names there is the greatest diversity in spelling; the word Miantonomo, or Miantonomi, has undergone more than twenty changes in orthography. To many of the citizens some of the facts will be entirely new; and to nearly all of them they will cast some light on what has passed away, and the various changes which have occurred during a period of two hundred and forty years.

HISTORICAL SKETCH.

FELLOW CITIZENS:

The choice of the Hon. Town Council has placed me in a rather delicate position, as I have not the gift of an orator, nor the ability of an historian; but I shall endeavor to present plain and unpolished truth, let its ennobling influence fall as it may.

In attempting to present on this occasion something of an historical sketch of this Town from its formation, for the approaching Centennial Anniversary of our National Independence of 1776, I shall not be overburdened with items of information, and of necessity must be brief.

The object for which this request of the General Assembly was made, is to draw forth from the fading archives of the past the original facts, and to collect the detached and scattered items, which are liable at any time to be lost, and to place them in a more durable condition, that future generations may avail themselves of these materials, when all other sources have been obliterated by the ravages of time.

The centennial monuments that mark the great advancement of civilization, from the time when Greece and Rome were celebrated for their genius in literature, philosophy, and fine arts, seem to point forward to the present period as the notable age of literary attainments and of wonderful inventions. This seems to be the language proclaimed by the leading men of all nations, that we are living in an inventive, progressive, and remarkable age. The researches of Newton, Fulton, Franklin, and Morse, have decided this point beyond a doubt, for they were eminent originators of mighty inventions, and their brilliant achievements will serve as guiding footsteps in ages yet to come. Nature has unveiled her hidden mysteries in a thousand different forms. Science has unlocked the doors of her ample store house of knowledge, and the nations of the earth are scattering the germs of usefulness promiscuously over this period of time in which we live. The people of Athens, in her splendor, were pre-eminently ahead of all other nations in art and literature ; and to her improvements may be added, for an illustration, the seven wonders of the world, which were the Egyptian Pyramids, the Mausoleum, the Temple of Diana at Ephesus, the Walls and Hanging Gardens of Babylon, the Colossus at Rhodes, the Statue of Jupiter Olympius, and the Watchtower of Alexandria ; yet these stupendous works of master minds have failed to produce such unlimited benefits for those nations as our modern inventions have furnished for the present and future generations of men.

The Steam Engine has become a thing of universal importance, exerting a prodigious power. They are applied to steamboats and steamships, which are plying on rivers, lakes and oceans, by thousands, against the fury of the winds and waves ; they are applied to the railway cars, which are traversing the countries in all directions, with the rapidity of the eagle in its flight ; they are applied to manufactories of almost every variety and kind, rendering cheap and accessible, all over the world, the material of wealth and utility ; and, finally, they are applied to the printing establishments, whereby the diffusion of intelligence and knowledge is increased with a power to which no limits can be assigned. The Telegraph is another noble and useful invention ; and in the language of the poet may we well exclaim :

> " It is a feat sublime,
> For intellect has conquered time."

On the 29th of May, 1844, the news of Mr. Polk's nomination was sent to Washington from Baltimore by the Magnetic Telegraph. It was the first dispatch ever so transmitted ; and the event marks an era in the history of civilization. The inventor of the telegraph, which has proved so great a blessing to mankind, was Professor Samuel F. B. Morse, of Massachusetts. We are certainly living in a marvelous and wondrous age, when New York and San Francisco are brought within four days of each other by travel, and entirely together by telegraphic communication. Mowing and Sewing Machines, which meet the wants of the present day, are among the great inventions of the nineteenth century. They have increased indefinitely the comforts and enjoyments of the human family ; and no person can fully contemplate the vast benefit to mankind conferred by these inventions, without thanksgiving and praise to the " Giver of All."

CONFIRMATORY DEED OF ROGER WILLIAMS AND HIS WIFE, OF LANDS TRANSFERRED BY HIM TO HIS ASSOCIATES, IN THE YEAR 1638.

Be it known unto all men by these Presents, that I, Roger Williams, of the Towne of Providence, in the Narragansett Bay, in New England, having in the yeare one thousand six hundred and thirty-four, and in the yeare one thousand six hundred and thirty-five, had severall treaties with Conanicusse and Miantonome, the chief sachems of the Narragansetts, and in the end purchased of them the lands and meadows upon the two ffresh rivers called Mooshassick and Wanasquatucket; the two said sachems having by a deed under their hands, two yeares after the sale thereof, established and conffirmed the boundes of these landes from the river ffields of Pawtuckqut and the great hill of Neotaconconitt on the northwest, and the towne of Moshapauge on the west, notwithstanding I had the frequent promise of Miantenomy, my kind friend, that it should not be land that I should want about these bounds mentioned, provided that I satisfied the Indians there inhabiting, I having made covenantes of peaceable neighborhood with all the sachems and natives round about us. And having, in a sense of God's merciful providence unto me in my distresse, called the place Providence, I desired it might be for a shelter for persons distressed of conscience ; I then, considering the condition of divers of my distressed countrymen, I communicated my said purchase unto my loving ffriends John Throckmorton, William Arnold, William Harris, Strikely Westcott, John Greene, senior, Thomas Olney, senior, Richard Waterman, and others, who then desired to take shelter here with me, and in succession unto so many others as we should receive into the fellowship and societye enjoying and disposing of the said purchase ; and besides the ffirst that were admitted, our towne records declare that afterwards wee received Chad Brown, William ffield, Thomas Harris, sen'r, William Wickenden, Robert Williams, Gregory Dexter, and others, as our towne booke declares. And whereas, by God's mercifull assistance, I was the procurer of the purchase, not by monies nor payment, the natives being so shy and jealous that monies could not doe it; but by that language, acquaintance, and favour with the natives, and other advantages, which it pleased God to give me, and also bore the charges and venture of all the gratuetyes which I gave to the great sachems, and other sachems and natives round about us, and lay ingaged for a loving and peaceable neighborhood with them, all to my great charge and travele ; it was, therefore, thought by some loving ffriends, that I should receive some loving consideration and gratuitye; and it was agreed between us, that every person that should be admitted into the ffellowship of injoying landes and disposing of the purchase, should pay thirtye shillinges into the public stock; and ffirst about thirtye poundes should be paid unto myselfe by thirty shillings a person, as they were admitted. This sum I received in love to my ffriends; and with respect to a towne and place of succor for the distressed as aforesaid, I doe acknowledge the said sum and payment as ffull satisffaction. And whereas, in the year one thousand six hundred and thirtye seaven, so called, I delivered the deed subscribed by the two aforesaid chiefe sachems, so much thereof as concerneth the aforementioned landes ffrom myselfe and my heirs unto the whole number of the purchasers, with all my poweres, right and title therein, reserving only unto myselfe one single share equall unto any of the rest of that number, I now againe, in a more fformal way, under my hand and seal, conffirm my fformer resignation of that deed of the landes aforesaid, and bind myselfe, my heirs, my executors, my administrators and assignes, never to molest any of the said persons already received or hereafter to be received into the societye of purchasers as aforesaid; but they, theire heires, executors, administrators and assignes, shall at all times quietly and peaceably injoy the premises and every part thereof; and I do ffurther, by these presents, binde myselfe, my heirs, my executors, my administrators and assignes, never to lay claime nor cause any claime to be laid, to any of the landes aforementioned, or unto any part or parcell thereof, more than unto mine owne single share, by virtue or pretence of any former bargaine, sale or mortgage, whatsoever, or joyntures, thirdes or intails made by me the said Roger Williams, or of any other person, either for, by, through or under me. In wittnesse thereof, I have hereunto sett my hand and seale this twentyeth day of December in the present year one thousand six hundred and sixty one.   ROGER WILLIAMS. [L. S.]

Signed, sealed and delivered, in presence of us,

THOMAS SMITH,

JOSEPH CARPENTER.

I, Mary Williams, wife unto Roger Williams, doe assent unto the premises. Wittness my hand this twentyeth day of December, in the present year one thousand six hundred and sixty-one.

The marke of M. W.   MARY WILLIAMS.

Acknowledged and subscribed before me.

WILLIAM FFEILD, *Generall Assistant.*

The lands transferred by Roger Williams to his associates were subsequently divided into what are called "home lots" and "six acre lots." In the clerk's office of the city of Providence is a revised list of lands and meadows as they were originally lotted, from the beginning of the plantation of Providence in the Narragansett Bay, in New England, unto the then inhabitants of the said plantation. The first in order are the "home lots," beginning at the "Mile-end Cove," at the south end of the town, between Fox Point and Wickenden-street. This book gives a list of fifty-four persons who "received their lots with their location." Here we find the founders of the State of Rhode Island. Their names are perpetuated and transmitted to us by pages of various histories; by inheritance of their numerous descendants; and finally, by being connected with the establishment of a colony among the Indians of North America, and the toleration of religious liberty.

A PARTIAL LIST OF THE FIFTY-FOUR NAMES.

Roger Williams,	William Wickenden,
William Harris,	John Lippitt,
John Greene,	Robert West,
William Arnold,	Joshua Winsor,
John Smith,	Thomas Hopkins,
Gregory Dexter,	John Sweet,
Chad Brown,	Edward Hart,
Daniel Abbott,	William Man,
Thomas Angell,	Francis Weston,
William Reynolds,	Richard Scott,
Thomas Olney,	Robert Cole,
William Carpenter,	Thomas James.

DEPOSITION OF ROGER WILLIAMS RELATIVE TO THIS PURCHASE FROM THE INDIANS.

NARRAGANSETT, 18 June, 1682.

I testify, as in the presence of the all-making and all-seeing God, that about fifty years since, I coming into this Narragansett country, I found a great contest between three sachems, two (to wit, Cononicus and Miantonomy) were against Ousamaquin on Plymouth side; I was forced to travel between them three, to pacify, to satisfy all their and their dependents' spirits of my honest intentions to live peaceably by them. I testify, that it was the general and constant declaration, that Cannonicus, his father, he had three sons, whereof Connonicus was the heir, and his youngest brother's

son Miantinomy (because of his youth) was his Marshal and Execu-
tioner, and did nothing without his unkle Cannonicus' consent.
And therefore I declare to posterity, that were it not for the favor
that God gave me with Cannonicus, none of these parts, no, not
Rhode Island, had been purchased or obtained, for I never got any
thing out of Cannonicus but by gift. I also profess that, being in-
quisitive of what root the title or denomination Nahiganset should
come, I heard that Nahiganset was so named from a little Island
between Puttisquomscut and Musquomacuk on the sea, and fresh
water side. I went on purpose to see it, and about the place called
Sugar Loaf Hill, I saw it, and was within a pole of it, but could
not learn why it was called Nohiganset. I had learnt that the
Massachusetts was so called from the Blue Hills, a little Island
thereabout; and Cannonicus' father and anchestors living in those
southern parts, transferred and brought their authority and name
into those northern parts all along by the sea side, as appears by the
great destruction of wood all along near the sea side; and I desire
posterity to see the gracious hand of the Most High, (in whose
hands is all hearts,) that when the hearts of my countrymen and
friends and brethren failed me, his infinite wisdom and merits stir-
red up the barbarous heart of Cannonicus to love me as his son to
his last gasp, by which means I had not only Miantonomy and all
the Cowesit sachems my friends, but Ousamaquin also, who, because of my great friendship with him at Plymouth, and the authority of Cannonicus, consented freely (being also well gratified by
me) to the Governor Winthrop's and my enjoyment of Prudence,
yea, of Providence itself, and all the other lands I procured of Cannonicus which were upon the point, and in effect whatsoever I desired of him. And I never denyed him nor Miantinomy whatever
they desired of me as to goods or gifts, or use of my boats or pin-
nace, and the travels of my own person day and night, which,
though men know not, nor care to know, yet the all-seeing eye hath
seen it, and his all-powerful hand hath helped me. Blessed be his
holy name to eternity.   R. WILLIAMS.

A PORTION OF A LETTER FROM ROGER WILLIAMS,
PRESIDENT OF PROVIDENCE COLONY, TO THE GEN
ERAL COURT OF MASSACHUSETTS, IN 1654.

Much Honored Sirs:

I truly wish you peace, and pray your gentle acceptance of a
word. I hope not unreasonable.

We have in these parts a sound of your meditations of war against these natives, amongst whom we dwell. I consider that war is one of those three great, sore plagues, with which it pleaseth God to affect the sons of men. I consider, also, that I refused, lately, many offers in my native country, out of a sincere desire to seek the good and peace of this.

I remember, that upon the express advice of your ever honored Mr. Winthrop, deceased, I first adventured to begin a plantation among the thickest of these barbarians. That in the Pequod wars, it pleased your honored government to employ me in the hazardous and weighty service of negotiating a league between yourselves and the Narragansetts, when the Pequod messengers, who sought the Narragansetts' league against the English, had almost ended that my work and my life together.

At my last departure for England, I was importuned by the Narragansett sachems, and especially by Ninigret, to present their petition to the high sachems of England, that they might not be forced from their religion, and, for not changing their religion, be invaded by war; for they said they were daily visited with threatenings by Indians that came from about the Massachusetts, that if they would not pray, they should be destroyed by war. With this their petition I acquainted, in private discourses, divers of the chief of our nation, and especially his Highness, who, in many discourses I had with him, never expressed the least title of displeasure, as hath been here reported, but after all hearing of yourself and us, it hath pleased his Highness and his Council to grant, amongst other favors to this colony, some expressly concerning the very Indians, the native inhabitants of this jurisdiction.

Now, with your patience, a word to these nations at war (occasion of yours,) the Narragansetts and Long Islanders, I know them both experimentally, and therefore pray you to remember—

First, that the Narragansetts and Mohawks are the two great bodies of Indians in this country, and they are confederates, and long have been, and they both yet are friendly and peaceably to the English. I do humbly conceive, that if ever God calls us to a just war with either of them, he calls us to make sure of the one to a friend. It is true some distaste was lately here amongst them, but they parted friends, and some of the Narragansetts went home with them, and I fear that both these and the Long Islanders and Mohegans, and all the natives of the land, may, upon the sound of a defeat of the English, be induced easily to join each with other against us.

The Narragansetts, as they were the first, so they have been long confederates with you; they have been true, in all the Pequod wars, to you. They occasioned the Mohegans to come in, too, and so occasioned the Pequods' downfall.

Their late famous long-lived Cannonicus so lived and died, and in the same most honorable manner and solemnity (in their way,) as you laid to sleep your prudent peace-maker, Mr. Winthrop, did they honor this their prudent and peaceable prince. His son, Mexham, inherits his spirit. Yea, through all their townes and countries, how frequently do many, and oft-times one Englishman, travel alone with safety and loving-kindness.

The cause and root of all the present mischief is the pride of two barbarians, Ascassassotic, the Long Island sachem, and Ninigret, of the Narragansett. The former is proud and foolish; the latter is proud and fierce. I have not seen him these many years, yet from their sober men I hear he pleads—

First, that Ascassassotic, a very inferior sachem, bearing himself upon the English, hath slain three or four of his people, and since that sent him challenges and darings to fight and mend himself. He, Ninigret, consulted by solemn messengers, with the chief of the English Governors, Major Endicott, then Governor of the Massachusetts, who sent him an implicit consent to right himself, upon which they all plead that the English have just occasion of displeasure.

After he had taken revenge upon the Long Islanders, and brought away about fourteen captives, divers of their chief women, yet he restored them all again, upon the meditation and desire of the English.

After this peace made, the Long Islanders, pretending to visit Ninigret, at Block Island, slaughtered of his Narragansetts near thirty persons, at midnight, two of them of great note, especially Wepiteamucoc's son, to whom Ninigret was uncle. All Indians are extremely treacherous; and if to their own nation, for private ends, revolting to strangers, what will they do upon the sound of one defeat of the English.

At a meeting of the Governor, Deputy Governor, and Assistants, held in Newport the 26th Nov., 1663, agreed and ordered, that John Sanford is chosen Clerke of this present meeting, to record the acts of this meeting, and till the Court of Election, and is in-gaged.

The Governor, Deputy Governor, and Council, having informed the Indians' Kings, viz., Quissuckquash and Nineganitt, that his gracious Majesty of England, having taken notice of the Narragansett Sachems submitting themselves subjects to his royall father, which submission they subscribed in writing and sent unto England by Mr. Gorton and others of Warwick, they owne that they did submitt themselves unto his Majesty's royall father, by a writinge under their hands about nineteene years ago; and they are now come to know what answer his Majesty is pleased to returne them. Alsoe, they owned that they sent a further declaration of their submission unto his Majesty by Mr. John Nickson, owning themselves therein his Majesty's subjects. As also they then, by the said Mr. Nickson, sent their humble petition unto his Majesty for reliefe in severall wrongs offered and done unto them by the other Colonies. The aforesayd submission sent by Mr. Gorton, being read in this meeting, and shewed to the sayd Sachems, they owned it their act.

It being informed unto the Narragansett Sachem Quissuckquash, that his Majesty of England hath graciously been pleased in our Pattent, to take the sayd Sachem and all the Narragansett Indians and lands into his gracious protection, as subjects unto himselfe: and also that his Majestye hath given this Colony ye government thereof, the sayd Sachem did voluntarily make answer that he most kindly thanked King Charles for his grace therein. It being also informed unto Nineganett, Sachem of the Nayantacott country, as was informed as aforesayd unto the Narragansett Sachem; he answered, that he most kindly thanked King Charles. The sayd Sachems being shewed aforesayd declaration and petition, sent by Mr. John Nicckson, they owned the same to be their act, and doe returne his Majesty great thanks for his gracious reliefe in releasinge their lands from those forced purchases and mortgages of theyr lands by some of the other Colonies.

PROCEEDINGS OF THE GENERAL ASSEMBLY HELD AT NEWPORT, THE 18TH DAY OF JUNE, 1817.

Will Davel, Indian, is ordered and allowed £3, out of the general treasury, for the loss of one of his eyes in the colony's service.

An Act enabling and appointing overseers to lease out the lands of Ninegret, the sachem, in the Narragansett country:

Whereas, Ninegret, the sachem of Narragansett lands in the colony of Rhode Island, &c., hath petitioned this Assembly to appoint three overseers, to oversee and rent out his lands, to prevent his being defrauded therein, and has also desired this Assembly to dispossess all those that shall refuse to hire of his overseers as shall be appointed by the Governor and company of said colony, for the time being ; and also, in case he hath need to sell any lands, that he may be, by the said Governor and company for the time being, assisted therein. For the complying with said petition, and for the better securing of the said sachem's lands and profits, be it there-fore enacted by this Assembly, and by the authority thereof it is enacted, that Col. William Wanton, of Newport, Major Thomas Frye, of East Greenwich, and Capt. Joseph Stanton, of Westerly, be, and they hereby are, appointed overseers to oversee and lease out said sachem's lands, as shall to them seem most conducive for the said sachem's interest ; empowering them, and they or any two of them, are hereby empowered, to dispossess all and every person that now is, or hereafter shall be, in possession of any said sachem's lands, and shall refuse to agree, comply and hire said lands at such rents and services as by them, or major part of them, shall be found most beneficial for said sachem's interest ; they not granting any lease for any longer term than seven years ; and the said sachem to pay the said charge thereof.

It is ordered by this Assembly, that Ninegret, sachem, have £10 lent him out of the general treasury, for two years ; and then to be paid by said Ninigret into the general treasury out of the rents of his lands.

PROCEEDINGS OF THE GENERAL ASSEMBLY, HELD AT NEWPORT, THE SECOND DAY OF MAY, 1718.

An Act to prevent Indians being sued for debt:

Whereas, several persons in this colony, out of wicked, covetous and greedy designs, often draw Indians into their debt, and take advantage of their inordinate love of rum, and other strong liquors, by selling the same to them, or otherwise to take advantages, by selling them other goods, at extravagant rates, upon trust, whereby said Indians have been impoverished, to the dishonor of the government. [Here follows the act. See public laws for 1719.]

PROCEEDINGS OF THE GENERAL ASSEMBLY, HELD AT NEWPORT, THE 17TH DAY OF JUNE, 1718.

Be it ordered, enacted and declared by this Assembly, and the authority thereof, that Ninegret, sachem, shall and do pass over and convey unto Cooke Ruffin's son, the land formerly granted his father, and to be under the same restriction as Ninegret's other lands are.

Whereas, an act of the General Assembly of this colony, made and passed at Newport, the 18th day of June, 1717, restricted the overseers of Ninegret, the sachem in Narragansett country, from leasing out any of the said sachem's lands for any longer time than seven years, the which hath been found prejudicial to the said sachem's interest, and hath much hindered the improvement of his lands ;

Be it therefore enacted by the General Assembly, and by the authority of the same, that the overseers of the land of the said Ninegret, sachem, shall and may have power to lease out the land of the said sachem for any term or time, not exceeding fourteen years, as to them shall seem most conducive for the said sachem's interest ; any act or clauses of acts to the contrary hereof, in any wise, notwithstanding.

PROCEEDINGS OF THE GENERAL ASSEMBLY, HELD AT NEWPORT, THE 23D DAY OF JUNE, 1724.

An explanation of an act of Assembly, exempting Indians from being sued for debt. [See public laws, 1730, p. 133.]

The trustees of Ninegret have paid into the general treasury £50, out of the money borrowed by said Ninegret of the colony.

There was paid into the general treasury of this colony, on the 13th day of June, 1727, the sum of £60, by Ninegret's trustees, the late sachem, in full of what was due from said sachem to this colony.

PROCEEDINGS OF THE GENERAL ASSEMBLY, HELD AT WARWICK, THE LAST WEDNESDAY OF OCTOBER, 1727.

This Assembly being informed that some persons have spread a report tending to the prejudice of the present constitution of this government, viz., that the General Assembly of this government is against the settling of a church, by any persons whatsoever, in the township of Westerly, which is false and groundless ;

It is enacted and declared, by the General Assembly of this Colony, that ten or twenty acres of land be laid out in the town of Westerly, out of the land of Ninegret, (he desiring the same,) for the erecting thereon a house for worship, according to the form of the church of England, or for erecting of a meeting house thereon (he desiring it,) for the use of any other society or societies ; and the trustees that are or shall be appointed to manage Ninegret's affairs by the government, to lay it out where they shall think it most convenient for a church or meeting house, upon said Ninegret's request.

Voted, that Ninegret's trustees render an account to the Assembly, at their next session, of the disposition of the monies received by them.

PROCEEDINGS OF THE GENERAL ASSEMBLY, HELD AT NEWPORT, THE FIRST WEDNESDAY OF MAY, 1731.

Voted, that Col. William Wanton, Major Thomas Frye, and Lieut. Col. Joseph Stanton, be a committee to survey several pieces of land in Westerly, which Ninegret, sachem, proposes to sell and dispose of, and make report to the next session of this Assembly.

PROCEEDINGS OF THE GENERAL ASSEMBLY, HELD AT NEWPORT, THE SECOND MONDAY IN JUNE, 1731.

Whereas, Col. Wanton, Major Thomas Frye, and Col. Joseph Stanton, were appointed a committee to survey several pieces of land, in Westerly, which Ninegret, Indian sachem, proposes to sell, and in pursuance thereunto, said committee having made report to this Assembly with three plats thereof;

It is therefore voted and ordered, that said report be accepted, and that said committee be still continued, and appointed to assist said Ninegret in selling said land, or any part thereof; and that notifications be set up in every town in this Colony forthwith, advertising of the sale of said land.

· And it is further ordered, that Ninegret, with the advice and con · sent of said committee, have full power to sell two acres of land that Stephen Wilcox formily bought of Ninegret, the late Indian sachem, deceased, where the iron works stood.

Whereas, Col. William Wanton, Major Thomas Frye, and Col. Joseph Stanton, (who were appointed to assist Ninegret, Indian sachem, in selling some lands,) presented a plat of said Ninegret's lands, containing three thousand one hundred and fifty-eight and three-quarter acres, dated the 14th day of June, 1731, a piece of said land taken off of the east corner of said plat, containing three hundred acres, which Col. Joseph Stanton purchased of the late Ninegret, Indian sachem, deceased, is ordered by this Assembly to be confirmed to the said Joseph Stanton.

PROCEEDINGS OF THE GENERAL ASSEMBLY, HELD AT EAST GREENWICH, THE 18TH DAY OF FEBRUARY, 1734-5.

Whereas, Charles Augustus Ninegret, sachem of the Narragansett Indians, by memorial to this Assembly, did set forth that there was an act of Assembly made and passed at Warwick, in the year 1727, ordering that ten or twenty acres of the memorialist's land should be laid out by a committee therein named, whereon to build a house for public worship, if the memorialist should desire the same; and in consequence thereof, the majority of the committee (the memorialist being present and desiring it) did mark out a convenient place for said purpose; upon which spot the members of the Church of England, in Westerly, did, at the memorialist's earnest desire, and at their proper charge, erect a house for public worship, in the way of the Church of England; but the land granted by the aforesaid act, for the said use, never having been laid out, nor properly conveyed by deed, the memorialist requested that twenty acres, at least, of his land be ordered forthwith to be laid out, and duly conveyed for the use of the Church of England, and in that part of it where said house or church is built;

Which being duly considered, be it enacted by the General Assembly, and by the authority of the same it is enacted, that Col. Joseph Stanton, Capt. John Hill, and Mr. William Babcock, or any two of them, be, and they are hereby, appointed and empowered to lay out twenty acres of land, as in the above memorial is prayed for; and that Ninegret be, and he is hereby, empowered to pass a deed for the due conveyance of the said twenty acres of land to the present minister of the Church of England, in Westerly aforesaid, and to his successors, to and for the use of said church, which deed, so passed, shall be good and valid in the law, for the purpose aforesaid.

PROCEEDINGS OF THE GENERAL ASSEMBLY, HELD AT WARWICK, THE THIRD MONDAY IN AUGUST, 1735.

Whereas, the inhabitants of the town of Westerly did, by petition, set forth to this Assembly, that they were destitute of a harbor there, by reason of the breach (that formerly used to be open in the largest salt pond in Westerly aforesaid) being shut or filled up; and at the time it used to be open, was but of little advantage to said inhabitants, because of the shallowness of the water in said breach; and as it is conceived, that by bringing or turning Pawcatuck river into said pond, it would be a means to cause said breach to continue open, and be much larger, and have more depth of water in it than it hath at any time heretofore had, so that the said pond would become a very commodious harbor, and navigable as well for small sloops as boats; and that it would be likewise very convenient for the catching and making of codfish, which would be of great service to this colony; but the cost and charge in carrying on said work would be more than the inhabitants of said town of Westerly were able to bear, and praying that this Assembly would assist them in defraying part of the charge in turning off the said river into said pond:

Which, being duly considered, it is therefore enacted by the General Assembly, that the said river be turned into the said pond, in order that the said breach may be opened; three-quarters of the charge whereof to be allowed and paid out of the general treasury: Provided, that the said town of Westerly, or any person in their behalf, will first procure and give sufficient bond to pay and discharge the other fourth part of the charge thereof; and also make and maintain such and so many bridges as there shall ever be occasion to make across said river, between the place where it is taken from its usual channel and the place where it will fall into said pond. And that Col. Joseph Stanton, Capt. Oliver Babcock, Mr. Samuel Perry, and Mr. Samuel Clarke, are appointed a committee to carry on the colony's part, and are empowered to draw money out of the general treasury as necessity requires.

PROCEEDINGS OF THE GENERAL ASSEMBLY, HELD AT NEWPORT, THE THIRD TUESDAY IN FEBRUARY, 1735 -36.

Voted and ordered, that Christopher Champlin, of Westerly, be, and he is hereby, appointed one of the committee for turning of Pawcatuck river (in the room of Capt. Oliver Babcock, who refuses.) And that those persons who appeared in behalf of the town of Westerly, viz., Col. Joseph Stanton, Mr. Christopher Champlin, Mr. Samuel Perry, and Mr. Samuel Clarke, be accepted and allowed of as sufficient bondsmen for said town, in case they give a bond of £2,000 to the general treasurer, according to the act of Assembly made for that purpose, for carrying on and bearing the one-quarter part of the charge of turning the above mentioned river, and making and maintaining all such bridges as shall be made over the same; and that if any others are willing to be bound with the above mentioned persons, they have the liberty.

Whereas, Messrs. Joseph Whipple, John Coddington, and Daniel Jenckes, who were appointed a committee to examine into the accounts of the trustees of the late Indian sachem, did report that they had audited the said accounts, and found that there was due to Col. Jos. Stanton the sum of £134 5s. 8d.; and also, that there were debts out-standing for lands sold, the sum of £150 2s. Whereupon it is voted and ordered, that the said report be accepted; and that the secretary take a copy of Col. Stanton's accounts, at the charge of the said sachem, and deliver the originals again to Col. Stanton.

PROCEEDINGS OF THE GENERAL ASSEMBLY, HELD AT NEWPORT, THE FOURTH TUESDAY IN AUGUST, 1738.

An Act for dividing and incorporating the town of Westerly into two towns, and the same to be known and distinguished by the names of Westerly and Charlestown.

Whereas, the present town of Westerly is .very large, and its inhabitants are numerous, many of whom live at a very remote distance from the place of meeting appointed for the transacting the public and prudential affairs of the town; and the rivers there (especially in the middle part thereof) being very large, so that the way to said meeting is rendered difficult as well as dangerous, and many of the inhabitants are thereby often impeded and hindered in attending thereon, which proves a great injury and hurt to them;

And whereas, the said town is well situated, and lies commodious for a division into two towns, which being divided, will tend to the general interest and advantage of all its inhabitants;

Be it enacted by the General Assembly of this colony, and by the authority thereof it is enacted, that the line for dividing said town be as follows, viz., beginning northerly, where Wood River enters the line between the said town of Westerly and North Kingstown, and so running by the natural course thereof, so far, until said river empties itself into a river called Pawcatuck; and then to run or extend as said Pawcatuck river runs by the banks thereof, westward, three miles; and from thence a south or southerly course, to the sea; and that, for the future, the town of Westerly extend no further eastward than the aforesaid line.

And be it further enacted, by the authority aforesaid, that all the rest of said lands heretofore Westerly, situate, lying and being to the eastward of the aforesaid line, be, and they are hereby, incorporated and erected a town, and called and distinguished by the name of Charlestown; and that the inhabitants thereof have all the liberties, privileges and immunities in the same manner as the other towns in the government enjoy by charters.

And be it further enacted by the authority aforesaid, that Jeremiah Gould, John Rice, and William Greene, Esqs., be appointed a committee to run a line between the aforesaid town, and erect and make thereon proper monuments and bounds for distinguishing the same, and to perform the same forthwith.

And be it further enacted, by the authority aforesaid, that the Justice of the Peace in the town of Charlestown, as soon as conveniently may be, issue forth a warrant, to summon in the freemen to elect and make choice of their town officers, for the management of the prudential affairs of said town ; and also, for the choice of two deputies for said town, to represent the same at the General Assembly in the October session next, and so on from time to time as by charter is appointed ; and that the town of Westerly send two deputies, to be chosen in manner as usual.

And be it further enacted, by the authority aforesaid, that each of the said towns have their proportion of the interest of the bank money appropriated for the towns in this colony, in the same proportion, and according to the sums that the lands in each town are mortgaged for.

And be it further enacted, by the authority aforesaid, that the town of Westerly send three grand jurors to attend on the general session of the peace for the county of Kings county, and two petit jurors to attend at the inferior court for said county ; and that the town of Charlestown send two grand jurors to attend on said court of general session of the peace, and two petit jurors to attend on said inferior court.

And it is likewise further enacted, that the towns of Westerly and Charlestown shall each send to the superior court one grand juror and one petit juror to attend on the same.

PROCEEDINGS OF THE GENERAL ASSEMBLY, HELD AT NEWPORT, THE THIRD TUESDAY IN SEPTEMBER, 1740.

Voted and resolved, that the Honorable Richard Ward, Esq., Governor, and Samuel Perry, Esq., be, and they are hereby, appointed trustees to Ninegret, sachem, in the room of the Honorable John Wanton, Esq., late Governor, and Col. John Potter, both deceased.

PROCEEDINGS OF THE GENERAL ASSEMBLY, HELD AT PROVIDENCE, THE 27TH OF OCTOBER, 1708.

At this session, the Assembly appointed Weston Clark, John Mumford of Newport, Phillip Tillinghast of Providence, Joseph Burden of Portsmouth, Richard Green of Warwick, and Captain John Eldred of Kingstown, a Committee to agree with Ninegret, " what may be a sufficient competence of land for him and his people to live upon," and to view the state of the Narragansett country.

In March, 1709, they reported that they had agreed with Nine-gret, and that they found a great deal of the land in the country there to be very poor, and some good. The deed of Ninegret is dated March 28, 1709, quit-claiming to the Colony all his title to the vacant lands, excepting a tract bounded as follows : " Begin-ning where the brook that Joseph Davill's mill standeth,* and runs into the great Salt Pond, and so from said brook on a strait line northerly to Pesquamscut Pond, and by the brook that runs out of Pesquamscut Pond into Pawcatuck river, and so along by Pawca-tuck river westward, until it comes to Benjamin Burdick's bridge, and from thence southerly towards Wequopogue, until it meets the grand road, and so along by said road eastward, until it comes near to Christopher Champlin's now dwelling house, and from thence south to the great pond or salt water, and so along by the pond side to the first mention bounds, as it is drawn out upon the draught of the vacant lands." [St. Rec. L. E. 3, 273.]

PROCEEDINGS OF THE GENERAL ASSEMBLY, HELD AT NEWPORT, THE FOURTH MONDAY IN JUNE, 1741.

Voted and resolved, that the trustees of Ninegret, sachem, render an account of their trust to the next session of this Assembly.

Whereas, George Ninegret, Indian sachem of the Narragansett

---

* Old Ninegret, who reserved this land for his tribe and himself, died somewhere about 1722. He gave to the colony a quit-claim deed of all his vacant lands, except a tract bounded as aforesaid: Beginning at the mouth of Cross' mill brook, (anciently known as Davill's,) where it empties into the salt pond, and thence from said brook on a straight line northerly to Pasquesett pond, and then along Pasque-sett brook until it joins the Pawcatuck river at Kenyon's Mills ; thence along the said river westward to Benjamin Burdick's bridge, (more recently called Brown's bridge at Burdickville ;) and thence southerly toward Wequopogue, a stream run-ning into Quonocontaug pond a little to the west of Quonocontaug Neck, and thence to the Post Road ; and then following said road eastward to Christopher Champlin's dwelling house, or very near it ; and from thence south to the salt pond, and so along the shore of said pond to the first mentioned bound.

Indians, humbly requested of this honorable Assembly to appoint George Wanton, of Newport, in the county of Newport, merchant, one of his overseers, he being well assured of his fidelity and justice in the management of his affairs ;

Whereupon, it is voted and ordered, that the said George Wanton be, and he is hereby, appointed a trustee or overseer to the said sachem, to have the same power in all respects with the other trustees.

PROCEEDINGS OF THE GENERAL ASSEMBLY, HELD AT SOUTH KINGSTOWN, THE FIRST DAY OF FEBRUARY, 1741–42.

Whereas, Rouse Helme, Esq., Messrs. Jeremiah Lippett and Job Tripp, Jr., were appointed a committee to audit the accounts of Col. Joseph Stanton, one of the trustees of the Indian sachem, and to make report thereon, which they accordingly did ; and reported that they found a balance due to the said Joseph Stanton of £142 12s. 3d., that he had advanced more than received, on account of the said sachem ;

Voted and resolved, that Mr. Samuel Perry be, and he is hereby, dismissed from being a trustee to George Ninegret, the Indian sachem, the said sachem having desired the same.

PROCEEDINGS OF THE GENERAL ASSEMBLY, HELD AT NEWPORT, THE 18TH DAY OF JUNE, 1745.

Whereas, George Ninegret, sachem of the Narragansett Indians, did represent to this General Assembly, that his late deceased brother, Charles Ninegret, (who was sachem of the said Narragansett Indians,) did, in his life time, give twenty acres of land as a glebe to and for the church of England, in Charlestown, in said colony ; but his said brother dying before he had made and executed a deed for the same, the said George Ninegret therefore requested leave of the General Assembly, that he might, by a proper deed for that purpose, establish said twenty acres to and for said church ; and also, to give and convey twenty acres more of his land, in said Charlestown, for the same use, in such place as shall be agreed on by himself and trustees ;

Upon consideration whereof, it is voted and enacted, that the said George Ninegret be, and he is hereby, allowed to pass a deed for the said twenty acres of land given by his said brother Charles

Ninegret ; and also for the twenty acres of land that he gives himself, to and for the use of the Church in Charlestown, aforesaid, in such place or places as he and his trustees shall think proper ; and that such deed or deeds, so given by him as aforesaid, shall be good and valid in the law, for the uses therein designed, to all intents and purposes whatever.

PROCEEDINGS OF THE GENERAL ASSEMBLY, HELD AT SOUTH KINGSTOWN, THE LAST WEDNESDAY OF OCTOBER, 1745.

An Act was passed allowing George Ninegret, the Indian sachem, to sell a part of his land, for the payment of his debts, and the better support of his family.

An Act empowering George Ninegret, the Indian sachem, (with the advice and consent of his trustees,) to exchange twenty acres of land in Charlestown, for the benefit of the Church of England, in that town.

PROCEEDINGS OF THE GENERAL ASSEMBLY, HELD AT NEWPORT, THE THIRD TUESDAY OF AUGUST, 1747.

An Act for incorporating the north part of the town of Charlestown, in King's County, into a township, the same to be distinguished and known by the name of Richmond :

Be it enacted by the General Assembly of this Colony, and by the authority thereof it is enacted, that the town of Charlestown, in the county of King's County, &c., be divided into two towns, by a river that runs across said town, known by the name of Pawcatuck River : all the lands to the southward of said river, shall retain the name of Charlestown ; and that all the lands to the northward of said river be, and hereby is, incorporated into a township, by the name of Richmond ; and to have and enjoy the like privileges as other towns in this colony.

And be it further enacted, by the authority aforesaid, that each of said towns shall have and receive a proportion of the money in and belonging to the treasury of said Charlestown, according to the money for which the lands in each town is mortgaged to the colony; and that all Justices of the Peace and military officers living within the bounds of said new town, called Richmond, retain their authority, and act as such therein, until the next general election; and that the eldest justice of each of said towns is hereby empowered to grant forth the warrants to some proper officer, whom they shall appoint to warn the inhabitants of said towns to assemble and meet together in some proper place, in said town, on Friday, the second day of this instant, August, in order to choose deputies to represent them at the October session of this Assembly, and also to choose town officers for said towns, agreeably to the laws of this colony; and that each town shall send one grand juror, and one petit juror, to each of the inferior and superior courts, in King's County.

Whereas, Sarah Ninegret, widow of George Ninegret, late sachem of the Narragansett tribe of Indians, deceased, and mother and natural guardian to Thomas Ninegret, an infant, the present sachem of said tribe of Indians, with Tobey Coheys, Samuel Niles, John Trask, William Sachem, Ephraim Coheys, Moses Hammond, James Niles, and Harry Copper, who were appointed by the said tribe of Indians councillors for the present sachem, Thomas Ninegret, in behalf of this sachem, themselves and people of said tribe of Indians, represented to this Assembly, that they, at the last sitting of this Assembly, in May last, did prefer a petition to said Assembly, setting forth the deplorable condition they are brought to by means of some gentlemen, namely, Joseph Whipple, Daniel Coggeshall, Samuel Perry, John Spencer, and David Anthony, Esqs., who, as they are informed, were appointed by the General Assembly, trustees, at its session, A. D. 1746, for the management of the rents and profits of the estate, said by some to be submitted to this government by the late Ninegret, sachem, deceased, in the year 1713; but without the desire, consent, request or knowledge of the said Sarah, and the said councillors or sachem, which was always usual, and such appointment was always at the request of the sachem and his council; and having set forth in said petition, that the said trustees, without the knowledge and consent of the sachem or any of the councillors, have leased out the land, which was always kept and reserved for the tribe of Indians, for planting of corn and raising other necessaries for their support. And the said Sarah and councillors further declared, that it is not only their fields and improvements, that they have fenced, and have been at great labor and charge in making said fences, that are rented out from them; but also, as they are credibly informed, the wood land, which was always kept and reserved for the tribe of Indians for fire wood ; and also the sachem's cedar swamp, is rented out, which was always kept and reserved for the tribe of Indians, to cut stuff and sell the same ; and the said Sarah and councillors apprehend that when the General Assembly appointed the above-named trustees, for the care and management of the rents and profits of the estate submitted to this government, in the year 1713, by the late Ninegret, sachem, deceased, that the General Assembly had no design nor intent to give the said trustees power to lease out the sachem's land without his knowledge and consent, and the knowledge and advice of his council ; and they likewise apprehended that the submission made by the sachem in the year 1713, (if any was made by him in that year,) doth not give the said trustees, or any others, power to lease out the sachem's land without his knowledge and consent ; they also informed this Assembly, that the gentlemen who were trustees to the late sachem, deceased, never leased out any of the said sachem's land without first having the leave and consent of the sachem and his council ; and as this Assembly have it in their power to relieve them in this their distressed condition, for they know not, as the case is, where to go, nor how to subsist themselves, and must be unavoidably starved without relief ;

Therefore, they humbly prayed that this Assembly would take their circumstances into consideration, and dismiss the above named trustees from their trusteeship, and make void all the leases given by said trustees of the sachem's land ; and that the Assembly would allow and accept of their known and trusty friends, Col. Joseph Stanton, Capt. George Wanton, and Capt. John Frye, to be trustees for the care and management of the sachem's estate, for the sachem's interest ; the last named gentlemen having been trustees to the late sachem ; and the said Sarah and councillors were knowing to the proceedings and management in that affair, and that their proceedings gave good satisfaction to the sachem, and a general satisfaction to the tribe of Indians, &c.

Upon consideration whereof, it is voted and resolved, that the prayer of the said Sarah and councillors be, and it is hereby, granted ; and that the said Joseph Whipple, Daniel Coggeshall, Samuel Perry, John Spencer, and David Anthony, be, and they are hereby, removed from their aforesaid office of trustees ; and that all the leases by them made, of the sachem's land, be, and they are hereby, declared and made null and void ; and the aforesaid Col. Joseph Stanton, Capt. George Wanton, and Capt. John Frye, are appointed trustees, for the care and management of the sachem's estate, for his interest.

PROCEEDINGS OF THE GENERAL ASSEMBLY, HELD AT SOUTH KINGSTOWN, THE LAST TUESDAY IN FEBRUARY, 1751-52.

Whereas, Col. Christopher Champlin, and Capt. Nathaniel Lewis, deputies of Charlestown, did, in behalf of said town, represent unto this Assembly, that they are under great difficulty and disadvantage, for want of some convenient harbor or landing, for transportation, it being about sixteen miles from said town to Point Judith Pier, and almost as far to Pawcatuck River, which places are the nearest harbors they have to depend on ; which they set forth to the General Assembly, some years past, who appointed a committee to inspect into the circumstances of said affair, and find out whether said difficulty might not be remedied by turning a branch of Pawcatuck River into a large salt pond in said town ; which stream of water (when turned into said pond) will undoubtedly keep open a large breach running out of said pond into the sea ; that the committee did view and examine into the affair, and reported to the Assembly, that it might be very well effected, and that without an extraordinary charge, &c. ; that upon the report of said committee, the Assembly, in their wisdom, passed an act for turning said river, for the purpose aforesaid, on conditions which were not easily to be performed by the petitioners ; they being to procure sufficient bonds to make and maintain such and so many bridges as should become necessary and occasioned by turning said river ; and also to carry on the fourth part of said work, the other three parts to be done at the charge of the colony ; that now the conditions enjoined by said act of Assembly are performed, &c ; whereupon, they prayed to be directed to go on in the aforesaid work, agreeably to the aforesaid act of Assembly ; and that the colony's part of the charge be paid out of the interests of the present bank, &c. ; and this Assembly having taken the premises into consideration, do vote and resolve, and it is voted and resolved, that Benjamin Hazard, Jeremiah Lippett, and Joseph Nichols, Esqs., together with Messrs. Joseph Harrison and Isaiah Wilkinson, be, and they, or the major part of them, are hereby appointed a committee, to inspect into all the circumstances relating to the aforementioned affair, and form an estimate of the cost and charge of performing said work, and report to this Assembly at their next session.

PROCEEDINGS OF THE GENERAL ASSEMBLY, HELD AT NEWPORT, THE SECOND MONDAY OF JUNE, 1753.

An Act for the relief of Charles Ninegret, sachem, an infant.

PROCEEDINGS OF THE GENERAL ASSEMBLY, HELD AT PROVIDENCE, THE 10TH DAY OF JANUARY, 1757.

The Hon. Stephen Hopkins, Governor, the Hon. John Gardner, Deputy Governor.

Whereas, Thomas Ninegret and several others, being part of the tribe of Indians living in Charlestown, preferred a petition, and represented unto this Assembly, that the said town of Charlestown, at a late quarter meeting, where but a small number of freemen were present, passed a vote obliging the said Indians to pay a part of the said town's proportion of the colony rate, which at this time is collecting ; and accordingly the rate makers have assessed them, and all the other Indians of the said town ; which being unusual, and, as they apprehend, a grievance, especially as they support their own poor without putting the town to any expense ; wherefore, they prayed to be relieved in such a way as may be thought proper ; on consideration whereof,

Be it enacted by this General Assembly, and by the authority thereof it is enacted, that the tribe of Indians aforesaid, be, and they are hereby, exempted from paying any share or part of the rate or tax aforesaid ; and that the rate makers of the said town of Charlestown be, and they hereby are, directed and required to assess that part of the said town's proportion upon the white inhabitants, that hath already been assessed upon the Indians of the said town. God save the King.

PROCEEDINGS OF THE GENERAL ASSEMBLY, HELD AT SOUTH KINGSTOWN, THE 14TH DAY OF FEBRUARY, 1758.

Whereas, the Rev. Joseph Park, of Charlestown, in the county of King's County, presented this Assembly with a memorial, setting forth that he hath been ever ready to contribute all the assistance in his power to repel His Majesty's enemies from their injurious encroachments on his dominions and just rights in North America, and to defend the country ; that in the year 1756, he consented to the voluntary enlistment of three of his sons, who served in the expedition formed for the reduction of Crown Point; that when they were discharged from the service, upon their return homeward, they put their clothing and other furniture, to the value of about £100, currency, in their chest, which was unfortunately lost in the sea ; that this summer, when the enemy attacked Fort William

Henry, they were substituted to go, and voluntarily went, in the stead of officers, who declined ; that they did this without any consideration, purely to serve their country, and oblige their friends ; that he, the memorialist, was thereby put to considerable charge, and received damage in his business ; wherefore, he prayed for such allowance as should be thought proper ; on consideration whereof,

This Assembly do vote and resolve, and it is voted and resolved, that the sum of £100 be paid the said Joseph Park, out of the general treasury, for the use of his aforesaid sons, as an allowance for what they lost, as aforesaid ; but that nothing be allowed them as officers.

PROCEEDINGS OF THE GENERAL ASSEMBLY, HELD AT EAST GREENWICH, ON THE 20TH DAY OF AUGUST, 1759.

An Act repealing all the laws of this colony, which restrict or prohibit the native Indians that live within the same, from disposing of their lands.

Whereas, Thomas Ninegret, of Charlestown, in the county of King's County, and colony aforesaid, gentleman, preferred a petition, and represented unto this Assembly, that having been unhappily engaged in several law suits, in defence of his right, he hath been obliged to advance large sums of money ; which, with other necessary expenses, he was put to for clothing, board, &c., during his minority, hath greatly involved him in debt ; and as the laws of the colony now stand, he cannot, in the apprehension of some, sell or dispose of his estate for the payment and discharge of his debts ; wherefore, he, the said Thomas Ninegret, prayed that the law which relates to the purchasing lands of Indians, may be repealed, and he have the same liberty of selling and disposing of his estate, or any part thereof, as others of His Majesty's subjects enjoy ; on consideration whereof,

Be it enacted by this General Assembly, and by the authority of the same it is enacted, that all and every of the laws at any time made and passed in this colony, to restrict or prohibit the native Indians, that live within the same, from selling and disposing of their estates, be, and they hereby are, repealed, declared and rendered null and void, to every intent and purpose, whatsoever.

PROCEEDINGS OF THE GENERAL ASSEMBLY, HELD AT EAST GREENWICH, THE 23D DAY OF FEBRUARY, 1761.

An Act for raising, by way of lottery, the sum of £20,000, in bills of credit, of the old tenor, to be appropriated for the turning one branch of the river called Pawcatuck River into the large pond in Charlestown.

Whereas, Thomas Ninegret, Christopher Champlin, and others, inhabitants of the county of King's County, preferred a petition, and represented unto this Assembly, that the inhabitants living in several of the towns in the southern parts of this colony, are put to great trouble and expense in transporting to market the produce of their farms by land, and bringing from market things necessary for their families; and whereas, there is in the town of Charlestown, a large pond, which may be made a good harbor for small vessels, and would be of great utility and advantage to the inhabitants, provided the communication of said pond with the sea could be kept open, which now is often interrupted; and whereas, the said petitioners are well advised that the turning of one branch of a river, called Pawcatuck River, into the said pond, would effectually keep open the said communication, so that small vessels at all times could with ease and conveniency pass from and into said pond, would not only answer the ends and purposes aforesaid, but would be of great advantage to the inhabitants, in carrying on the codfishery, &c.

Here follows the act and scheme of the lottery. The directors named in the act were Robert Potter, Gideon Hoxsey, John Champlin, Joseph Hoxsey, John Congdon, and Samuel Burdick, Jr.

PROCEEDINGS OF THE GENERAL ASSEMBLY, HELD AT NEWPORT, ON THE SECOND MONDAY OF JUNE, 1763.

Whereas, a considerable number of the Narragansett tribe of Indians, within this Colony, preferred a petition, and represented unto this Assembly, that the land belonging to the said tribe of Indians, which was reserved by old Ninegret, the Narragansett sachem, was by him reserved to and for his use, and the use of his said tribe and their children, forever; that a law was passed in this Colony, to make void all grants, deeds and leases made by the sachem of said tribe, without the consent and approbation of the

General Assembly ; that the said law, although it had been long in force, and proved very beneficial to said tribe, hath been lately repealed ; in consequence whereof, Thomas Ninegret, the present sachem, hath, without the approbation of the General Assembly, or consent of said tribe, sold and conveyed away divers tracts of land belonging to said tribe, and is daily so doing ; by reason whereof, a great part of said tribe are in danger of being utterly deprived of the means of procuring a maintenance, and must either starve or become a town charge ; and thereupon, the petitioners prayed this Assembly to pass an act to prohibit the said sachem from selling any more of said lands from them, (especially their particular settlements,) without the consent, as formerly, of his tribe, and of the General Assembly ; and that until they can be heard by this Assembly, the said sachem may be restricted from selling any of said lands. On consideration whereof,

It is voted and resolved, that this petition be referred to the next session ; that Thomas Ninegret, the present sachem of said tribe, be served with a copy thereof, and cited to appear at the next session, to answer the same ; and that in the mean time, the said Thos. Ninegret be, and he is hereby, restricted and forbid to sell and dispose of any lands in the Narragansett country, upon any pretence whatever.

PROCEEDINGS OF THE GENERAL ASSEMBLY, HELD AT NEWPORT, ON THE FIRST MONDAY IN AUGUST, 1763.

Whereas, a number of the Narragansett tribe of Indians, in this Colony, preferred a petition to this Assembly, at the last session, which was referred to the present session ; on consideration whereof,

It is voted and resolved, that Joseph Lippitt, Thomas Church, Job Randall, and John Barker, Esqs., and Mr. William Potter, be, and they are hereby, appointed a committee, to set off and bound the various tracts of land that heretofore have been appropriated, by the sachems of the Narragansett tribe of Indians, to that tribe, for their sole use, maintenance and support ; he, the sachem of said tribe, agreeing and consenting to give and execute a good and effectual deed to said tribe ; and also liberty of passing and repassing on his lands to the pond and sea, for the advantage of fishing ; which the petitioners, in presence of the upper house of Assembly, agreed to accept of.

PROCEEDINGS OF THE GENERAL ASSEMBLY, HELD AT NEWPORT, ON THE SECOND MONDAY OF JUNE, 1764.

Whereas, Joseph Lippitt, Thomas Church, Job Randall, and John Barker, Esqs., presented unto this Assembly the following report, to wit:

Report of the Committee concerning the lands of the Narragansett tribe of Indians:

We, the subscribers, with Mr. William Potter, being appointed by the Honorable General Assembly, at their session in August last, to set off and bound the various tracts of land that heretofore have been appropriated by the sachems of the Narragansett tribe of Indians to that tribe, for their sole use, maintenance and support, &c., do report: That, agreeably to said appointment, we have been and viewed the said lands; and on examining said Indians, and others, cannot find any lands set off or appropriated by the sachems to said tribe as a tribe; but we find various tracts or pieces of land, which have been set off to particular persons or families, amounting, in the whole, to between two and three thousand acres; which, the sachem saith, is what he meant to give and execute a deed of to said tribe, and is still willing to do it, according to his agreement and promise at said General Assembly; but as there are large tracts of land, which are neither leased by the sachem, nor set off to any of the tribe, but seem to be in common, used when wanted, both by sachem and tribe, the petitioners insisting on that, or part of it, being set off with the rest. And whereas, there is a larger number of said tribe than the petitioners, who seem utterly against being set off, but choose to remain with the sachem, as heretofore; and say the petitioners may be set off by themselves, but they are not willing to be set off with them; but we not having authority to set off any lands to part of the tribe, unless we could have persuaded them to agree where and how much; so, after several days waiting on them, trying to get them to agree how much to set off, and where, but we could not, we were obliged to return, and do report as above said.

All which is submitted by Joseph Lippitt, Thomas Church, Job Randall, John Barker.

N. B. As the lands set off and improved by the tribe, or particular persons, are intermixed with other lands, some leased, and others unimproved, we think, if it be set off from the other lands, it must be surveyed, which is a work of considerable time.

PROCEEDINGS OF THE GENERAL ASSEMBLY, HELD AT NEWPORT, ON THE LAST MONDAY IN JUNE, 1767.

Whereas, a letter was laid before this Assembly, from Andrew Oliver, Esq., to His Honor the Governor, respecting a school house erected on the Indian lands, in the Narragansett country ;

It is thereupon voted and resolved, that Thomas Ninegret, sachem of the Narragansett tribe of Indians, be notified by a citation from the secretary, directed to some proper officer, to appear at the next session ; and that, in the mean time, he do not by any means dispose of any of his lands ; and that His Honor the Governor be, and he is hereby, requested to write to Mr. Oliver, and inform him of this vote.

PROCEEDINGS OF THE GENERAL ASSEMBLY, HELD AT SOUTH KINGSTOWN, THE LAST WEDNESDAY IN OCTOBER, 1767.

It is voted and resolved, that Joseph Hazard, Daniel Coggeshall, James Helme, Benjamin Peckham, and Freeman Perry, Esqs., be, and they, or the major part of them, are hereby appointed a committee, to advertise all persons who have any demands on Thomas Ninegret, sachem of the Narragansett tribe of Indians in this colony, to bring in the same, upon oath, to the said committee; who, with the assistance of the said sachem, and five of his council, are empowered to settle his accounts, and ascertain what is justly due to each person ; and also to sell and dispose of so much of the Indian lands as may be sufficient to discharge the just debts, and also the charges arising on this affair. Provided, nevertheless, that the said committee shall inquire into his personal estate, and apply so much thereof as they shall think proper, for the payment of said debts, before they proceed to the sale of the lands.

And it is further voted and resolved, that the said sachem be, and he is hereby, forever hereafter restricted from selling any more of said lands ; and that the same shall not be chargeable for any debts he shall hereafter contract.

This Assembly, taking into consideration the letter from Andrew Oliver, Esq., laid before this Assembly at the last session, do vote and resolve, and by and with the consent of Thomas Ninegret, sachem of the Narragansett tribe of Indians, in this colony, it is voted and resolved, that the said Thomas Ninegret, and five of his council, make, execute and give, to the secretary of this colony, a good and legal deed of an island in a certain swamp, in Charles-

town, in this colony, containing about three acres, whereon stands a
school house, for the use of a school for said tribe of Indians, forever ; with the privilege of a convenient passage to and from the
same ; that Matthew Robinson, Esq., be, and he is hereby, appointed to draw the same deed, and see the same executed ; and that
the whole charge accruing thereon be paid by said tribe.

PROCEEDINGS OF THE GENERAL ASSEMBLY, HELD AT PROVIDENCE, THE LAST WEDNESDAY IN OCTOBER, 1768.

It is voted and resolved, that Thomas Ninegret, sachem of the
Narragansett tribe of Indians, in conjunction with five of his councilors, be allowed to sign, and in common form to execute, a deed
or deeds, to any person or persons, of so much land, belonging to
him and his said tribe, as will be sufficient to pay and discharge all
his debts, as settled and allowed by the committee of this Assembly, in the October session, in the year 1767 ; thereby conveying
to said purchaser or purchasers an estate in fee simple ; that as
well the quantity of land so to be conveyed, be allowed by said
committee, as also that the said committee do approve of the con-
veyances, by signing said deeds, certifying under their hands, that
they approve of the same. And it is the design and intent of this
Assembly, that none of those lands may be taken, sold and disposed of by the aforesaid sachem and his councilors, that are in the
actual possession and under the particular separate improvement of
any particular Indian or Indians, which they hold and use as their
private parts or possessions. And it is further voted and resolved,
that the said committee, or the major part of them, be, and they
are hereby, authorized and empowered to take and receive all further claims and demands of debts which were contracted before the
October session of the Assembly, in the year 1767, or from any of
the creditors of the said sachem, within one month after the rising
of this Assembly, and not after. And also said committee is hereby empowered to take and receive of and from the purchaser or
purchasers of said lands, to be sold, as aforesaid, all and every sum
and sums of money arising from the sale thereof, to and for the
use of the said creditors of said sachem; and to pay said creditors
their respective debts ; therewith taking full discharges therefor,
from each creditor for his respective debt or debts ; and that the
said committee be paid for their trouble out of said money rising
from said sale, as this Assembly shall hereafter direct and order ;

and the said committee render an account of their doings thereon, to this Assembly.

PROCEEDINGS OF THE GENERAL ASSEMBLY, HELD AT EAST GREENWICH, ON THE LAST MONDAY IN FEBRUARY, 1769.

Upon the petition of Thomas Ninegret, sachem of the Narragansett tribe of Indians, and six of his council—

It is voted and resolved, that Joseph Hazard, Daniel Coggeshall, James Helme, Sylvester Robinson, and Freeman Perry, Esqs., be, and they, or the major part of them, are hereby, appointed a committee, to complete the settling of the accounts of Thomas Ninegret, sachem of the Narragansett tribe of Indians, in this colony, with the assistance of five of his council; and to sell and dispose of so much of the Indian land as will be sufficient to discharge his just debts; that therein they follow the directions and orders of this Assembly, as contained in the votes of the General Assembly relating to said matters, at their session in October, 1767, and October, 1768, with this addition, that they immediately proceed upon that business, and complete the same within three months after the rising of this Assembly; and that they have full power therein, and the same allowance therefor as the committee appointed by said votes heretofore made and passed.

PROCEEDINGS OF THE GENERAL ASSEMBLY, HELD AT NEWPORT, ON THE SECOND MONDAY OF JUNE, 1769.

It is voted and resolved, that James Helme, Joseph Hazard, and Sylvester Robinson, Esqs., be, and they are hereby, appointed a committee, to sell and dispose of the real estate of Thomas Ninegret, Indian sachem, for the payment of his debts: and the same to do in three months from the rising of this Assembly, agreeably to the restrictions and votes already passed for that purpose.

PROCEEDINGS OF THE GENERAL ASSEMBLY, HELD AT EAST GREENWICH, ON THE SECOND MONDAY IN SEPTEMBER, 1769.

Whereas, James Daniel, William Sachem, David Phillip, Henry Harry, and Christopher Harry, the council of Thomas Ninegret, sachem of the Narragansett tribe of Indians, preferred a petition,

and represented unto this Assembly, that the committee appointed
to make sale of the real estate of said Thomas Ninegret, for the
payment of his just debts, have sold some of the said lands; that
it appears that the whole of his debts cannot be paid without selling a piece of land called and known by the name of Fort Neck;
one part of which lies to the southward, and the other to the northward, of the post road; that part lying to the southward being all
the land belonging to the said Thomas Ninegret that joins to the
Salt Pond, upon which all the said tribe depend for their fishing;
that when the committee were disposing of the land of the said
Thomas Ninegret, he, together with the petitioners, considering
that the tribe principally depended upon the fishery for a living,
wanted to dispose of the said piece of land, called Fort Neck, to
such person or persons as would be agreeable to them; but that
the committee, being of opinion that the said land must be disposed of at public sale, could not allow them that privilege, and adjourned to the 27th day of this instant, September; and therefore
they prayed this Assembly to grant them the liberty to sell and
dispose of the said piece of land, called Fort Neck, to such person
or persons as shall be agreeable to them, under the care and inspection of the said committee, and at the value of the said land.

And whereas, the petitioners further represented, that since the
order of Assembly for selling the estate of the said Thomas Ninegret, for the payment of his debts, he hath contracted other debts
for his necessary subsistance: and if it had not been for the favors
he received from some particular friends, must have suffered; that
every person to whom he owed any sum which could be brought to
a justice's court, hath sued him, and he hath been obliged to make
over every thing he hath of personal estate, even to the clothes on
his back, to prevent his going to jail for his small debts; and that
unless a sufficient quantity of land be sold to pay the small demands against him, he must immediately go to jail; and thereupon
they further prayed, that the said committee may be empowered to
sell a sufficient quantity of land to pay the just debts contracted
by the said Thomas Ninegret since the General Assembly have re-
strained him from disposing of his estate; the demands against
him being under the same inspection of the committee as those
demands which were against him before the act of Assembly so re-
straining him. And the premises being duly considered—

It is voted and resolved, that the committee appointed at the
last session, to sell and dispose of the real estate of Thomas Ninegret, Indian sachem, for the payment of his debts, be, and they are
hereby, continued a committee for that purpose; and empowered

to complete the same, within three months after the rising of this Assembly.

And it is further voted and resolved, that the said committee be, and they are hereby, empowered, with the consent of the said sachem and five of his council, to sell a sufficient quantity of the said sachem's lands to pay all the just debts he now oweth.

And it is further voted and resolved, that the petitioners be, and they are hereby, empowered to sell and dispose of the said piece of land, called and known by the name of Fort Neck, to such person or persons as they shall think proper, either at public or private sale; the money arising from the sale thereof to be paid to the committee, and to be appropriated to the payment of the said sachem's debts; and the deeds of the estate or estates which shall be sold in pursuance of this act, shall be made and given in the same manner as is directed by an act of this Assembly, passed in October, A. D. 1768, appointing a committee to sell and dispose of the estate of the said Thomas Ninegret, for the payment of his debts.

PROCEEDINGS OF THE GENERAL ASSEMBLY, HELD FOR THE COLONY OF RHODE ISLAND AND PROVIDENCE PLANTATIONS, AT SOUTH KINGSTOWN, ON THE LAST MONDAY IN FEBRUARY, 1770.

Whereas, Esther Sachem, (calling herself queen of the tribe of Indians in this colony,) Thomas Sachem, her husband, and Henry Harry, with others, as her council, who preferred a petition unto this Assembly, praying that she, with her husband and council, and James Helme, Joseph Haszard, and Sylvester Robinson, Esqs., (who were a committee appointed by this Assembly, to dispose of the estate of Thomas Ninegret, deceased, late sachem of said tribe, for the payment of his debts,) may make a deed or deeds of the estate of the said Thomas Ninegret, for the payment of his just debts, in the same manner as the said Thomas Ninegret, in his life time, with his council, and the said committee, by act of Assembly, might have done; and whereas, Samuel Niles and others, (calling themselves a council, appointed by said tribe, for transacting their public affairs,) did appear before this Assembly, and for the settlement of the disputes and differences subsisting in said tribe, did mutually agree that the Hon. Joseph Wanton, Esq., the Hon. Stephen Hopkins, Esq., and Joseph Haszard, Esq., or any two of them, by their consent, and by order of this Assembly,) should be empowered to inquire into the subject matter of their disputes, and in

particular to ascertain and to set off all the lands which shall, upon
inquiry and examination, appear to them to have been the lands or
estates of the said Thomas Ninegret, deceased, for the payment
and satisfaction of the debts due to his creditors and to his heirs,
after such debts as are paid and satisfied ; that the expense of such
inquiry and examination be equally paid by the said two parties ;
and that the said report be made to this Assembly at the next session ; and the premises being duly considered ;

Be it enacted by this General Assembly, and by the authority
thereof it is enacted, that the above recited agreement be, and hereby is, approved ; and that the said Joseph Wanton, Stephen Hopkins, and Joseph Haszard, or any two of them, be empowered to do
and transact every thing submitted to them by said agreement.

And be it further enacted, by the authority aforesaid, that the
above-named James Helme, Joseph Haszard, and Sylvester Robinson, or any two of them, be empowered to take into their care and
possession all such lands as shall be set off as the estate of the
said Thomas Ninegret, deceased, and the same to improve, in such
a manner as they shall think most for the interest of his heirs and
creditors, until so much of them shall be disposed of as will be sufficient to satisfy and pay his just debts. God save the King.

PROCEEDINGS OF THE GENERAL ASSEMBLY, HELD
FOR THE COLONY OF RHODE ISLAND AND PROVI-
DENCE PLANTATIONS, AT NEWPORT, ON THE SEC-
OND MONDAY IN JUNE, 1770.

Whereas, Esther Sachem and Thomas Sachem preferred the following petition unto this Assembly, to wit:
Petition of Esther Sachem, and her husband, to the General Assembly, relative to Thomas Ninegret, late sachem of the Narragansett tribe of Indians :
To the Honorable General Assembly, to be holden at Newport,
in the county of Newport, on the second Monday of June, A. D.
1770, humbly show Esther Sachem of Charlestown, in King's
county, who is heir-at-law to Thomas Ninegret, sachem of the Narragansett tribe of Indians, together with her husband, Thomas
Sachem, that the General Assembly did take the affairs of her deceased brother into their care, long before his death, and appointed a committee to take an account of his debts, and dispose of so
much of his lands as would discharge the debt against him ; who
proceeded so far as to take an account of his debts, and to dispose

of a small part of his lands ; when the General Assembly interpos-
ed, and appointed a new committee, to set off what did belong to
the sachem, that should be sold to discharge the debts against the
estate ; which said committee have done nothing ; that, as the
affair hath been several years in this situation, the creditors to said
estate are uneasy, and the principal part of said estate is under a
heavy mortgage, and unless the General Assembly orders something to be immediately done, all the creditors will sue at the August court ; and that the mortgage is now in suit, and hath been
continued two terms, and must be yielded up at the rising of the
August court, unless the affair can be settled before ; besides, the
debts are upon interest, and increase fast, which, with the charges
of two law suits, will swallow up the whole estate, if speedy reme-
dy be not taken.

Therefore, they humbly pray the General Assembly to take their
distressed circumstances into consideration, and order the last appointed committee to proceed immediately, and set off what lands
shall be sold ; and upon their setting off said land, that the former
committee immediately proceed to dispose of the lands, and pay the
demands against the estate, so far as the General Assembly have
ordered them to be paid.

And they, as in duty bound, will ever pray.

ESTHER SACHEM, her ╳ mark.
THOMAS SACHEM, his ╳ mark.

July 11th, 1770.

On consideration whereof, it is voted and resolved, that the foregoing petition be, and hereby is, granted.

PROCEEDINGS OF THE GENERAL ASSEMBLY, HELD FOR THE COLONY OF RHODE ISLAND AND PROVIDENCE PLANTATIONS, AT EAST GREENWICH, ON THE SECOND MONDAY IN SEPTEMBER, 1770.

The Hon. Joseph Wanton, Governor ; the Hon. Darius Sessions,
Deputy Governor.

Whereas, the Hon. Stephen Hopkins, Esq., and Joseph Haszard,
Esq., presented unto this Assembly the following report, to wit :

Report of the Committee appointed by the General Assembly, relative to the affairs of the Narragansett tribe of Indians :

We, the subscribers, being appointed a committee, by the General Assembly, to inquire into some disputes subsisting among the
Narragansett tribe of Indians, and to endeavor to settle the same,
do report :

That we repaired into the Indian country, convened all the principal Indians there before us, and prevailed with them all to agree, that as much of their land may be sold as will pay the late sachem Thomas' debts; provided, that no land be sold for that purpose but such as the tribe shall appoint; and that the General Assembly pass an act, that no more of the Indian lands may be sold afterwards, upon any pretence whatsoever.

The Indians requested that the committee appointed to adjust the sachem Thomas' debts may be empowered to examine for what the debts became due, notwithstanding they may now be reduced to mortgages, bonds, notes, &c., suggesting great impositions therein. The Indians further requested, that the General Assembly would appoint two of them to be Justices of the Peace, for punishing drunkenness, breach of the peace, and other offences amongst themselves. Then the Indians pointed out the following parcels of land to be sold:

1. The large house the late sachem Thomas lived in, with twenty-six acres of land adjacent to it.

2. The house the late sachem George dwelt in, with about sixty acres of land about it.

3. A tract of land, heretofore sold at vendue to Isaac Nye, but not yet measured, nor any deed given.

4. A small piece of land in possession of James Perry.

5. A small piece of land in possession of Joseph Hoxsie.

6. Nine acres and a half of land lying by a place called Wellshare.

And lastly, as much of the Cedar Swamp as will complete the payment of Thomas' debts.

Finally, the Indians did agree and promise to provide as good a support for the remaining branches of the royal family, as the small remains of their public lands, and the loyal affections of a poor people, can admit.

All which agreements and requisitions we promised the Indians to recommend to the General Assembly as fit to be confirmed and granted. And we do accordingly recommend them as worthy the notice and approbation of the General Assembly, and presume to subscribe ourselves,

' Their faithful servants,

STEPHEN HOPKINS,
JOSEPH HASZARD,

East Greenwich, Sept. 10th, 1770.

And the said report being duly considered, it is voted and re-solved, that the same be, and hereby is, accepted and approved ; excepting that part thereof recommending it to the General Assem-bly to appoint Indian Justices of the Peace, which is disapproved by this Assembly.

It is further voted and resolved, that the several pieces and par-cels of land and estates mentioned in the said report, be sold for paying the late sachem Thomas' debts ; and that no other of the Indian lands be thereafter sold, on any pretence whatever.

It is further voted and resolved, that the committee appointed to adjust the said sachem Thomas' debts, and to sell the lands for payment thereof, be, and they are hereby, empowered to examine how the debts became due, notwithstanding they may now be re-duced to mortgages, bonds, notes, or judgments of courts, which have been obtained by default ; that no more of said debts be paid than shall appear to be justly due ; and that the said committee be, and they are hereby, empowered to defend against all actions that have been, or shall be, brought against the late sachem Thomas' estate ; and that all expenses and costs attending the defending in any action brought, or that may be brought, against the said estate, shall be defrayed out of the said estate.

And it is further voted and resolved, that the Hon. Stephen Hopkins, Esq., be, and he is hereby, added to the committee ap-pointed to adjust the debts of the said Thomas, to examine how they became due, and to sell and dispose of the lands for the pay-ment thereof.

PROCEEDINGS OF THE GENERAL ASSEMBLY, HELD AT PROVIDENCE, ON THE LAST MONDAY IN OCTOBER, 1770.

Whereas, this Assembly, at their session in October, 1767, passed an act, appointing Matthew Robinson, Esq., to draw a deed, to be executed by Thomas Ninegret, late sachem of the Narragansett tribe of Indians in this colony, and five of his council, to the Sec-retary, of an island in Charlestown, for the use of a school for the said tribe of Indians, and to see the same executed, &c., as by the said act will appear ; and whereas, the said Thomas Ninegret hath since deceased without having executed the said deed ;

It is therefore voted and resolved, that the said act be revived, and that the present Queen of said tribe, with five of her council, be, and they are hereby, fully empowered to make, execute and give such a deed as in the said act is mentioned.

PROCEEDINGS OF THE GENERAL ASSEMBLY, HELD AT NEWPORT, THE FIRST WEDNESDAY OF MAY, 1771.

Whereas, the General Assembly did heretofore appoint the Hon. Stephen Hopkins, Esq., James Helme, Esq., Joseph Haszard, Esq., and Sylvester Robinson, Esq., a committee, they, or the major part of them, to settle and adjust the accounts and demands of the creditors of Thomas Ninegret, late sachem of the Narragansett tribe of Indians, in this colony, and to assist in the sale of so much of his lands as would discharge his debts, and the necessary expense attending said affair; and whereas, the said sachem is since deceased, and proper deeds of sundry tracts of land bargained and sold for that purpose were not in the life-time of said sachem duly made and executed to the purchasers of said lands, Be it therefore enacted by this General Assembly, and by the authority of the same it is enacted, that the aforesaid committee, or the major part of them, together with the council of the said late sachem, or the major part of them, make and execute deeds of so much of the lands of said sachem as will be sufficient for the purpose aforesaid.

PROCEEDINGS OF THE GENERAL ASSEMBLY, HELD AT NEWPORT, THE FIRST WEDNESDAY OF MAY, 1772.

Whereas, Henry Harry, Christopher Harry, James Daniel, Samuel Niles, James Niles, Ephraim Coheas, Thomas Lewis, John Shattock, and Joseph Tucky, the council for the tribe of Narragansett Indians, in this colony, represented unto this Assembly, that they are all of opinion it will be best to sell the little house, and the two acre lot, and the wood lot, (the exact quantity not being ascertained,) and as much of Fort Neck as will pay all Thomas Ninegret's just debts; and that they are all of one mind, to sell so much of Fort Neck as will pay those debts, and to reserve the lands which will be left to support all their poor; in consideration whereof,

It is voted and resolved, that the committee appointed to sell a part of the real estate of Thomas Ninegret, the late sachem, for the payment of his debts, proceed to do the same, agreeably to the above-mentioned proposal.

PROCEEDINGS OF THE GENERAL ASSEMBLY, HELD AT PROVIDENCE, ON THE SECOND MONDAY IN DECEMBER, 1772.

Whereas, two of the council of the Narragansett tribe of Indians, in this colony, are dead, and William Sachem (one of the said council) refuseth to sign the deeds for the sale of the lands of Thomas Ninegret, deceased, late sachem of the said tribe ;

It is therefore voted and resolved, that the committee appointed to settle the estate of the said Thomas Ninegret, with two of the surviving council of the Indians, make and execute a deed or deeds of the lands they have already sold, or may hereafter sell, to pay the said Ninegret's debts ; and that such deed or deeds be as good and valid, to all intents and purposes, as though the said deed or deeds had been made and executed by the committee and all the Indian council.

PROCEEDINGS OF THE GENERAL ASSEMBLY, HELD AT NEWPORT, ON THE THIRD MONDAY IN AUGUST, 1773.

Whereas, the following petition, signed by forty-three Indians of the Narragansett Tribe in this colony, was presented unto this Assembly, to wit :

Petition of the Narragansett Tribe of Indians to the General Assembly.

To the Honorable the General Assembly of His Majesty's colony of Rhode Island, holden at Newport, the third Monday of August, 1773, the petition of us, the subscribers, Indians of the Narragansett Tribe, in said colony, humbly showeth :

That some of our late sachems, through extravagance and indiscretion, had heretofore run themselves largely in debt ; and for the discharging those debts we have consented to the sale of the greatest part of the most valuable lands belonging to the tribe ; so that there now remaineth only one small piece of Fort Neck, by which they can get to the salt water, from which they fetch great part of the support of themselves and families. And being informed by the honorable committee appointed by the Assembly to settle the accounts and discharge the debts of the late sachem Thomas Ninegret, deceased, that they apprehend that they, with our consent, have sold lands sufficient to discharge the whole of said debts ; we therefore humbly petition this honorable Assembly to pass an act to secure to the said tribe, forever, as well the said small part of Fort Neck, as all the other lands now of right belonging to them ; and that the same be not, for the future, liable to the payment of debts.

We would further represent to this honorable Assembly, that when the late sachem Ninegret, by his deed of the 28th of March,

1709, in consideration of the protection of the colony, resigned to
the Governor and Company of said colony, the lands then called
the vacant lands, he, by the same deed, excepted and reserved to
himself, for the use of the tribe, a certain tract of land, bounded
on the east as followeth, that is to say: "Beginning at the brook
where Joseph Davil's mill standeth, and runs into the Great Salt
Pond; and so, from said brook on a straight light, northerly, to
Pasqueset Pond, and by the brook that runs out of Pasqueset
Pond into Pawcatuck River." That soon after, and while the intent of the parties was well known, by order and direction of the
late Col. Joseph Stanton, and others of the committee appointed
by the General Assembly to oversee the Indian affairs, the line was
run from the said brook to Pasqueset Pond, and bounds made.
That afterwards, some persons, who claimed lands to the eastward
of said line, caused another line to be run from the most western-
most parts of said brook, viz: Cross' Mill Dam, to Pasqueset
Pond. By the running of which last mentioned line, as well the
burying ground and graves of our ancient sachems and fathers, as
also several hundred acres of land, which were not intended to be
granted by the deed aforesaid, are claimed, and, against right, held
from the Indians, by sundry persons in Charlestown. We, therefore, humbly pray this honorable Assembly to authorize and em-
power the committee for settling the affairs of the late sachem
Thomas Ninegret, or some one or more of them, to cause an exact
survey of the said lines, and so much of the brook and Pasqueset
Pond as may be necessary to illustrate the facts, to be taken; and
that a draught thereof be laid before this honorable Assembly, for
their advisement thereon.

And we do, on this occasion, approach the General Assembly
with the greater confidence, because we look upon them as our
guardians and protectors, agreeably to the consideration of the
sachem Ninegret. The granting our prayer will oblige your petitioners, as in duty bound, ever to pray, &c.

And the said petition being duly considered, it is voted and resolved, that the same be, and hereby is, granted; that all the lands
now of right belonging to the said tribe, be secured to them; and
that the same, or any part thereof, shall not, for the future, be liable
to the payment of any debts. That James Helme, Esq., or some
other of the committee appointed for settling the accounts of the
late sachem Thomas Ninegret, cause a survey of the lines of the
lands claimed by the said tribe, and the lands claimed by some
other persons in Charlestown, and held from the said tribe (as it is
said in the said petition) against right; that a draught of the same

be laid before this Assembly at the next session; that he be, and hereby is, empowered to summon and swear witnesses respecting the same. That the secretary cause notifications to be set up in one or more public places in Charlestown, notifying the persons claiming said lands, to appear before the next session of Assembly, to be then heard thereon: and that the colony be at no charge respecting this affair, but that the charge thereof be paid by the said tribe.

AID TO THE POOR OF BOSTON.

On the 20th of Dec., 1774, Joseph Hoxsie and Christopher Babcock were appointed a committee to receive donations of the people of Charlestown, consisting of sheep and money, and to transmit the same to a committee chosen by the town of Boston. This committee were authorized to receive donations for the relief of those who were suffering by the reason of the Act commonly called the "Boston Port Bill." On the last day of March, 1774, the Boston Port Bill was passed by Parliament. It was enacted, that no kind of merchandise should any longer be landed or shipped at the wharves of Boston. The custom-house was removed to Salem, but the people of that town refused the benefits which were proffered by the hand of tyranny. To what extent the generosity of the inhabitants of Charlestown was extended to the people of Boston, I do not know; but it is gratifying to understand, that something was done to mitigate the sufferings of the people. During this period, the little girl in Connecticut sent her pet lamb, with a ribbon tied around its neck, to the poor of Boston. This has been the poets' theme, and many pieces have been written about Mary's little lamb.

THE PEQUOT INDIANS.

The Pequots occupied the neighborhood of New London, Groton and Stonington, with the Mohegans on the north of them. Sassacus, their sachem, had a strong fort between New London and Mystic River. The Pequots were considered to be the most warlike and cruel of all the New England tribes. The terrible murders perpetrated by them, and the awful tortures which they inflicted upon their English captives, were sure warnings to the white people, that something must be speedily done to check them, or the colonists would be totally annihilated.

On the first day of May, 1637, the General Court of Connecticut, assembled at Hartford, declared war against the Pequots, raised an army of ninety men, and appointed Captain John Mason command-er-in-chief of the expedition. The soldiers were enlisted, and sailed from Hartford, May 10th, 1637, accompanied by Uncas and seventy friendly Indians. The little fleet, which consisted of three vessels, met adverse winds, and finally sailed into Narragansett Bay. Here, on Tuesday evening, May 23d, the gallant little band landed, and immediately set out for the residence of Miantinomo. Mason marched the next morning, May 24th, for the Pequot fort. As he proceeded on his journey, he was reinforced by a large party of Narragansetts sent on by Miantinomo. Their line of march from Narragansett was along the old Indian path, traveled from time immemorial by the Indians, and which was the great highway for all the travel from Boston, and the north and east, to Connecticut and New York; following the course of the shore, perhaps very near the route of the present Post Road, through Tower Hill, Wakefield, Charlestown and Westerly. Mason reached the Niantic Fort* the next evening, May 24th, which he sur-

---

*THE NIANTIC FORT.

The Niantic Fort, alluded to by Capt. Mason during his famous march from Nar-ragansett Bay, near Wickford, to Westerly, in 1637, was built on Fort Neck, which is about twelve miles to the east of Westerly, and perhaps eighty rods to the south-west of Cross' Mills. The land has steep banks on the south side, next to the water, and it projects into Pawaget or Charlestown Pond. The remains of the old fortress are still visible, with traces of ditches, and a wall of stone and earth. It was torn down by the white people, and the larger part of the stones used in build-ing a wall to inclose the land. This fort contained three-fourths of an acre, and appears in the form of a square. There were three bastions, twenty feet square, one on each of three angles or corners, which completely covered the ditches and walls of the fort. It appears that the main entrance to the fort was reached at the south corner, near the pond, and the only corner without a bastion. On the 24th of May, 1637, while Mason and his troops halted here, it was then garrisoned by a large body of the Niantics, who would not allow any of Mason's men to enter the fortification. Undoubtedly, it was a strong and well fortified position. Here, then, is one particular instance on record, in which the condition of the Niantic fort was known to the English.

SHUMUNCANUC FORT.

There is now to be seen, in the western part of Shumuncanuc, on the land known as the George N. Crandall estate, and between Watchaug Pond and Burdickville, the remains of an old fortress, which resembles very much the one erected at Fort Neck, both in size and construction; but unlike the former in one respect, it had no bastions. The probability is, that these two forts were designed and construct-ed by the same tribe. This fort measured sixty yards square, and inclosed three-fourths of an acre of land. Tradition informs us, that this fort was built by the Niantics, as a protection to their fishing privileges, and a defense against the Pe-quots. The remains of this work are now faintly visible, and in a few years more, they will be removed by the ravages of time beyond the recognition of man. It was in this locality that the sachem Ninegret, who died soon after King Philip's war, or about the year 1676, lived and exercised kingly sway over his subjects. On his death, his first daughter succeeded him, and the ceremonies of her inaugura-

rounded until morning, to prevent any treachery by the Niantics,
when, after a fatiguing march of twelve miles, he reached the ford-
ing place in Pawcatuck river. After dinner, Mason continued his
march on to Taugwonk, in Stonington. Here he halted, and learn-
ed for the first time, that the Pequots had two very strong forts.
He, however, resolved to move on and attack the fort at Mystic.
The guides brought them to the fort, two hours before light, May
26th, 1637. Mason went forward, and when within a rod of the
fort, was discovered by a Pequot, who cried out, "Owanux! Owanux!" Englishmen! Englishmen!

A hand to hand contest ensued; the wigwams and fortress were
set on fire; and at this time the destruction was terrible beyond
any human description. The number thus destroyed was about
400, the result of which was the complete overthrow of the Pequots
as a tribe, and the consequent salvation of the English settlement
on the Connecticut river. The English, in their retreat, were
attacked by the enemy from the other fort at Weinshawks, but re-
pulsed them with great slaughter. It was estimated that six or
seven hundred perished in this fire and fight. Sassacus, their
great sachem, fled to the Mohawks, who put him to death at the
instigation of the Narragansetts. Thus the Pequot nation passed
away.

THE NARRAGANSETT SACHEMS.

Canonicus was the Grand Sachem of the Narragansetts when the
whites settled at Plymouth. History gives no account of his pre-
decessors. It commences with him. He died June 4th, 1647.
Miantinomo was his nephew, son of his brother Mascus. Canonicus, in his advanced age, admitted Miantinomo into the government, and they administered the sachemdom jointly. In the war
between the Narragansetts and Mohegans, in 1643, Miantinomo
was captured by Uncas, the Sachem of the Mohegans, and executed. Pessecus, the brother of Miantinomo, was then admitted Sachem with Canonicus. He was put to death by the Mohawks, in
1676. Canonchet, the son of the brave but unfortunate Miantinomo, was the last Sachem of the race. He commanded the Indians

---

tion took place at Chemunganock, which is now changed to Shumuncanuc. After
the death of the Queen, her half brother Ninegret succeeded her, and reigned until his death, or about 1722. The Niantics, their wigwams and their fortresses, have
been swept away from the earth. We can now clearly understand, from the wild
and romantic appearance of the country, that the advantages for hunting and fishing, which induced the poor Indians to dwell here, were far superior to those of
any other.

at the Great Swamp Fight, in 1675. This battle exterminated the Narragansetts as a nation. He was captured near the Blackstone River, after the war, and executed for the crime of defending his country, and refusing to surrender the territory of his ancestors by a treaty of peace. It was glory enough for a nation to have expired with such a chief. The coolness, fortitude, and heroism of his fall stands without a parallel in ancient or modern times. He was offered life upon the condition that he would treat for the submission of his subjects; his untamed spirit indignantly rejected the ignominious proposition. And when he was told his sentence was to die, "he said he liked it well, that he should die before his heart was soft, or he had spoken any thing unworthy of himself." His head was cut off, and sent to Hartford. The rest of his body was burnt. This ended the last chief of the Narragansetts, and with Canonchet the nation was extinguished forever.

THE ROYAL HEADS OF THE NIANTIC TRIBE.

Ninigret was the Sachem or Sagamore of the Nyantics, or the Westerly Tribe, and since the division of that town, now styled the Charlestown Tribe. Ninigret was tributary to Canonicus, Miantinomo, and his successors. He was only collaterally related to the family of Canonicus; Quaiapeu, Ninigret's sister, having married Maxanno, the son of Canonicus. The whites purchased Ninigret's neutrality, during the Indian war of 1675, and for his treachery to his paramount sovereign and his race, the "Tribe Land" in Charlestown was allotted to him and his heirs forever, as the price of the treason. The Ninigret Tribe never were the real Narragansetts, whose name they bear. It is a libel on their glory, and their graves, for them to have assumed it. Not one drop of the blood of Canonicus, Miantinomo, or Canonchet, ever coursed in the veins of a Sachem who could sit neuter in his wigwam, and hear the guns and see the conflagration ascending from the fortress that was exterminating their nation forever. Ninigret died soon after the war. From this Ninigret, the succeeding Indian Sachems were descended. By one wife he had a daughter, and by another he had a son, Ninigret, and two daughters; one of which is sometimes designated as the Old Queen. On Ninigret's death, the first-named daughter succeeded him, and the ceremonies of her inauguration took place at Chemunganock, now known as Shumuncanuc. These ceremonies were the presentation of peage and other presents, as an acknowledgment of authority; and sometimes a belt of peage was publicly placed on the Sachem's head, as an ensign of rank. On

her death, her half brother Ninigret succeeded. He died some
where about 1722. His Will is dated 1716–17. He left two sons,
Charles and George Augustus Ninigret. The former succeeded as
Sachem, and dying, left an infant son Charles, who was acknowledged as Sachem by a portion of the tribe, but the greater part ad-
hered to George, his uncle, as being of pure royal blood. The dis-
pute was encouraged by different white people, who wished to obtain an influence over the tribe, and to purchase their lands; and
seems to have been ended only by the death of young Charles.
George Augustus was acknowledged as Sachem in 1735. He left a
widow and three children, Thomas, George and Esther.

On Thursday, the 6th of Sept., 1750, the bans of marriage being
duly published at the church of St. Paul's, in Narragansett, no ob-
jection being made, John Anthony, an Indian man, was married to
Sarah George, an Indian woman, the widow and Dowager Queen of
George (Augustus) Ninigret, deceased, by Dr. McSparran. Thomas (commonly known as King Tom) was born in 1736, and succeeded as Sachem in July, 1746. While he was Sachem, much of the
Indian land was sold, and a considerable part of the tribe emigrated to the State of New York, and joined the Indians there.

William Kenyon, late of Charlestown, deceased, in a statement to
Wilkins Updike, says: "I knew King Tom Ninigret; he had a
son named Tom, his only child. He went away, and died before
his father. Tom's brother George having died, the crown descended to Esther, the next heir. I (continued Mr. Kenyon) saw her
crowned, over seventy years ago. She was elevated on a large rock,
so that the people might see her; the council surrounded her.
There were present about twenty Indian soldiers with guns. They
marched her to the rock. The Indians nearest the royal blood, in
presence of her councillors, put the crown on her head. It was
made of cloth, covered with blue and white peage. When the
crown was put on, the soldiers fired a royal salute, and huzzaed in
the Indian tongue. The ceremony was imposing, and every thing
was conducted with great order. Then the soldiers waited on her
to her house, and fired salutes. There were 500 natives present,
besides others. Queen Esther left one son, named George; he
was crowned after the death of his mother. I was one of the jury
of inquest, (continues Mr. Kenyon,) that sat on the body of George.
He was about 22 years old when he was killed. He was where
some persons were cutting trees. One tree had lodged against
another, and in cutting that one it fell, and caught against a third,
and George, undertaking to escape, a sharp knee struck him on the
head, and killed him; a foot either way would have saved him,

No King was ever crowned after him, and not an Indian of the whole blood now remains in the tribe."

Thomas Ninigret, who was better known as King Tom, was born in 1736, and succeeded as Sachem in July, 1746. At the age of ten years, he was crowned king of the Niantics. He received a common school education in England, where he was sent by his nation; and on his return from school, he brought a draft of a house with him; and soon afterward built the structure known as the Sachem house, which served him as a dwelling place during the remainder of his days. It is commonly reported among the people, that Thomas Ninigret was a large, fleshy man; that he had an uncommon appetite for strong drink; and that he became a confirmed inebriate toward the last years of his life. His wife, and Thomas Ninigret, his only son, left him and emigrated to the West. Idleness and intemperance soon reduced him to poverty and wretchedness. His authority was denied him; his friends deserted him; and, in brief, the most of his property passed out of his hands to cancel his debts. He died some time between the second Monday in September, 1769, and the last Monday in February, 1770. Very soon after his death, a considerable portion of the tribe lands was sold to defray his expenses. The King's mansion was purchased by Nathan Kenyon, Esq., and from him it descended to James Kenyon, his son, and finally to James Nichols Kenyon, his grandson, the present proprietor.

Esther Ninigret, the only sister of Thomas Ninigret, married Thomas Sachem; and by him she had a son named George, who met with a tragical fate. The coronation of Queen Esther occurred as early as 1770, according to the best information that can be obtained. The rock on which she was elevated by her friends and councilors, preparatory to the reception of the crown, is situated about twelve rods to the north of the late Thomas Ninigret's residence. It is an isolated rock, projecting about three feet above the ground, well adapted to such occasion; and it has become famous for this event.

George Sachem, who met a premature death by a tree falling upon him, was the son of Queen Esther. The place, which has often been pointed out to me, where he was killed, is located about sixty rods to the north of the school house pond, and at nearly the same distance from the child-crying rocks. I cannot understand, from any source, that he was ever crowned, although Mr. Wm. Kenyon, of Charlestown, made the assertion many years ago. But in his death, when his sun went down to rise no more, the nation's last and final hope expired.

CHARLESTOWN, HOPKINTON AND RICHMOND.

The Towns of Charlestown, Hopkinton and Richmond were formerly included in the township of Westerly. The town of Westerly was incorporated in 1669, and was then the fifth town in the Colony of Rhode Island.

An act was passed, August 22d, 1738, by the General Assembly, held at Newport, dividing the town of Westerly into two towns, the same to be known and distinguished by the names of Westerly and Charlestown. At this period, Charlestown extended from Westerly on the west, to South Kingstown on the east; and from the town of Exeter on the north, to the Atlantic Ocean on the south.

But on the 18th day of August, 1747, an act was likewise passed dividing the town of Charlestown into two divisions, to be distinguished by the names of Charlestown and Richmond; and the Pawcatuck River was selected as a natural and fixed boundary between the two towns. At the first census, taken in 1748, Charlestown had a population of 1,002; and in 1774 a population of 1,821; while the present population, according to the last census, taken in 1875, is 1,054.

At the first Town Meeting held in Charlestown, Sept. 4th, 1738, the following officers were elected:

Moderator—Justice Samuel Perry.

Town Clerk—Wm. Clark, who held that office from 1738 to 1747, the year in which Richmond Town was set off from Charlestown.

Town Council—Col. Joseph Stanton, Capt. Wm. Clark, Capt. John Hill, John Hoxsie, Capt. Daniel Stanton, Justice Samuel Wilbur.

Town Treasurer—John Hoxsie.

Town Sergeant—Nathaniel Potter.

Constables—James York, John Kenyon, Jr.

Assessors of Taxes—Capt. John Hill, Justice Samuel Perry.

Overseers of the Poor—John Hoxsie, Thomas Stanton.

Town Surveyor—Joseph Stanton, Jr.

1st Deputy—Col. Joseph Stanton.

2d Deputy—Samuel Perry.

Surveyors of Highways and Fence Viewers—Thomas Stanton, Isaac Sheffield, Joseph Clark, Joseph Hoxsie, John Kenyon, John Webster.

Flax Viewers—Thomas Stanton, John Hoxsie, Joseph Eanos, Isaac Sheffield, Wm. James.

Viewer of Codfish, Bone and Oil—Henry Green.

Sealer of Weights and Measures, and Packer of Fish—William Bently.

Grand Juror—John Knowles.

Petty Juror—Wm. King.

The following is a list of persons who hold office at the present time, July 4th, 1876 :

Senator—Hon. George C. James.

Representative—Hon. Charles Cross.

School Committee—Elisha S. Peckham, Chairman ; John A. Wilcox, M. D., Clerk ; Wm. F. Tucker, Superintendent.

Surveyors of Highways—

Dist. No. 1. Nathan K. Foster.	Dist. No. 12. Jason P. Green.
2. Stanton S. Green.	13. Bowen Briggs, Jr.
3. Samuel Browning.	14. Jesse B. Reynolds.
4. Horace Wilcox.	15. George F. Burdick.
5. Benj. Tucker.	16. Charles D. Ennis.
6. George W. Kenyon.	17. Charles Burdick.
7. Thomas Johnson.	18. James W. Hoxsie.
8. Green Card.	19. B. D. Macomber.
9. Gardner W. Sullivan.	20. Gideon P.G.Hoxsie.
10. Elisha S. Peckham.	21. David C. Kenyon.
11. Amos P. Greene.	22. Edward T. Burdick.
23. Joseph A. Sullivan.	

Town Clerk—Charles Cross.

Moderator—James N. Kenyon.

Town Council—Stephen C. Browning, Gardner W. Sullivan, Wm. Greenman, George F. Burdick, Jason P. Green.

Justice of the Peace, or Trial Justice—Oliver D. Clark.

Town Treasurer—George H. Ward.

Town Sergeant—Joseph C. Church.

Constables—John Congdon, Varnum Ennis.

Overseer of the Poor—Hazard G. Kenyon.

Surveyors of Lumber—Caleb Kenyon, Benj. Tucker.

Assessors of Taxes—Charles Holden, Hazard G. Kenyon, Newman B. Card, Stanton T. Stedman, James A. Kenyon.

Sealer of Weights and Measures—Charles Cross.

Pound Keeper—Reuben A. Healy.

Field Driver—Asa Noyes.

Packers of Fish—Benj. B. Green, Charles M. Burdick.

Auditors of Town Treasurer's Accounts—Charles Cross, John A. Wilcox, M. D.

Town Surveyors—Archibald Barber, Caleb Kenyon.

Wreck Masters—George H. Ward, Horace Wilcox.
Auctioneers—Henry C. Card, John Congdon, Joseph E. Taylor.

February Term of Supreme Court:

Grand Juror—Beriah C. Kenyon.
Petty Juror—Franklin E. Brown.

May Term of Court of Common Pleas:

Grand Juror—Benjamin B. Green.
Petty Juror—Henry S. Green.

Appointed by the Governor, at the May Session, A. D. 1876:

Commissioner of the Narragansett Indians—John A. Wilcox, M. D.
Commissioner of the Indian School—Wm. F. Tucker.

LIST OF PERSONS WHO HAVE HELD THE OFFICE OF TOWN CLERK, FROM SEPT. 4TH, 1738, TO 1876.

William Clark, September 4th, 1738, to September, 1747.
Joseph Stanton, Jr.,   "   "   1747,   "   "   1753.
Robert Potter,   "   "   1753,   "   "   1755.
Joseph Hoxsie,   "   "   1775,   "   "   1760.
John Champlin,   "   "   1760,   "   "   1761.
Gideon Hoxsie,   "   "   1761,   "   "   1762.
John Champlin,   June, 1762, to November, 1763.
Joseph Hoxsie,   November, 1763,   to   June,   1769.
James Congdon, 3d,   June, 1769,   "   "   1772.
Joseph Stanton, Jr.,   "   1772,   "   "   1773.
James Congdon, 3d,   "   1773,   "   "   1783.
John Champlin,   "   1783,   "   "   1785.
Col. Peleg Cross, Jr.,   "   1785,   "   "   1787.
Benjamin Hoxsie, Jr.,   "   1787,   "   "   1791.
Col. Peleg Cross, Jr.,   "   1791,   "   "   1817.
Samuel Stanton,   "   1817,   "   "   1838.
John Stanton,   "   1838,   "   "   1847.
William H. Perry,   "   1847,   "   "   1849.
Gideon Hoxie, Jr.,   "   1849,   "   March, 1851.
John Stanton,   March, 1851,   "   June, 1852.
Charles Cross,   June, 1852,   "   "

LIST OF PERSONS WHO HAVE HELD THE OFFICE OF TOWN TREASURER, FROM SEPT. 4TH, 1738, TO 1876.

John Hoxsie, from 1738 to 1739.
Samuel Wilbur, from 1739 to 1742.
Joseph Eanos, from 1742 to 1744.

Samuel Wilbur, from 1744 to 1745.
Joseph Eanos, from 1745 to 1747.
Benjamin Hoxsie, from 1747 to 1755.
John Hill, Jr., from 1755 to 1756.
Benjamin Hoxsie, from 1756 to 1758.
Gideon Hoxsie, from 1758 to 1760.
Benjamin Hoxsie, from 1760 to 1761.
Gideon Hoxsie, from 1761 to 1762.
John Champlin, from 1762 to 1764.
Joseph Hoxsie, from 1764 to 1778.
Benjamin Hoxsie, Jr., from 1778 to 1783.
Robert Congdon, from 1783 to 1788.
Tobias Saunders, from 1788 to 1789.
Jonathan Hazard, Jr., from 1789 to 1791.
Tobias Saunders, from 1791 to 1796.
Robert Congdon, from 1796 to 1801.
Nathan Taylor, from 1801 to 1802.
Christopher Saunders, from 1802 to 1818.
Hoxsie Perry, from 1818 to 1826.
Peleg Cross, from 1826 to 1833.
George W. Cross, from 1833 to 1864.
Preserved Davis, from 1864 to 1867.
George W. Cross, from 1867 to 1871.
George H. Ward, from 1871 to

GENERAL ASSEMBLY.

MEMBERS OF THE HOUSE OF DEPUTIES.

FIRST DEPUTY.	SECOND DEPUTY.	WHEN ELECTED.
Col. Joseph Stanton,	Samuel Perry,	Sept. 4th, 1738.
Samuel Perry,	Capt. Wm. Clark,	March 6th, 1739.
" "	Capt. Isaac Sheffield,	July 6th, 1739.
" "	Capt. John Hill,	March 4th, 1740.
Samuel Wilbur,	Christopher Champlin,	August 28th, 1740.
Samuel Perry,	Joseph Church,	March 3d, 1741.
Capt. Joseph Stanton,	Capt. Chris. Champlin,	August 25th, 1741.
Samuel Perry,	" " "	March 2d, 1742.
Wm. Clark, Jr.,	Nathaniel Lewis,	August 31st, 1742.
Maj. Chris. Champlin,	Capt. Nathaniel Lewis,	March 1st, 1743.
Stephen Hoxsie,	John Webster,	August 30th, 1743.
" "	Col. Chris. Champlin,	April 18th, 1744.
John Hicks,	Wm. Clark, Jr.,	August 28th, 1744.
Col. Joseph Stanton,	Joseph Hicks,	April 7th, 1745.

FIRST DEPUTY.	SECOND DEPUTY.	WHEN ELECTED.
James Congdon,	Samuel Perry,	August 27th, 1745.
Richard Bailey,	" "	April 18th, 1746.
Col. Chris. Champlin,	Wm. Clark, Jr.,	August 26th, 1746.
Col. Joseph Stanton,	" "	April 15th, 1747.
" "	James Congdon,	August 27th, 1747.
" "	" "	April 28th, 1748.
Col. Chris. Champlin,	Capt. Nathaniel Lewis,	August 28th, 1748.
Col. Joseph Stanton,	James Congdon,	April 19th, 1749.
Capt. Nathaniel Lewis,	Benjamin Hoxsie,	August 29th, 1749.
James Congdon,	Capt. Nathaniel Lewis,	3d Wed. April, 1750.
Col. Chris. Champlin,	" " "	last Tues. Aug. 1750
" "	" " "	3d Wed. April, 1751.
" "	" " "	last Tues. Aug. 1751
" "	" " "	3d Wed. April, 1752.
Capt. Nathaniel Lewis,	James Congdon,	last Tues. Aug. 1752
Capt. Joseph Stanton,	Col. Chris. Champlin,	3d Wed. April, 1753.
" "	" "	last Tues. Aug. 1753
Col. Chris. Champlin,	Robert Potter,	3d Wed. April, 1754.
" "	" "	last Tues. Aug. 1754
" "	Capt. Joseph Stanton,	April 16th, 1755.
James Congdon,	Nathaniel Sheffield,	last Tues. Aug. 1755
Col. Chris. Champlin,	Capt. Robert Potter,	3d Wed. April, 1756.
" "	Gideon Hoxsie,	last Tues. Aug. 1756
" "	" "	April 20th, 1757.
Capt. Robert Potter,	Joseph Hoxsie,	August 30th, 1757.
" "	" "	3d Wed. April, 1758.
" "	Peleg Cross,	last Tues. Aug. 1758
" "	Col. Chris. Champlin,	3d Wed. April, 1759.
Gideon Hoxsie,	Joseph Hoxsie,	last Tues. Aug. 1759
Col. Chris. Champlin,	Capt. Robert Potter,	3d Wed. April, 1760.
" "	" "	last Tues. Aug. 1760
" "	" "	3d Wed. April, 1761.
Joseph Stanton,	Capt. John Champlin,	last Tues. Aug. 1761
Capt. Robert Potter,	" "	3d Wed. April, 1762.
" "	" "	last Tues. Aug. 1762
" "	" "	3d Wed. April, 1763.
" "	" "	last Tues. Aug. 1763
" "	Col. Chris. Champlin,	3d Wed. April, 1764.
" "	Gideon Hoxsie,	last Tues. Aug. 1764
" "	Joseph Hoxsie,	3d Wed. April, 1765.
" "	John Congdon,	last Tues. Aug. 1765
" "	Gideon Hoxsie,	3d Wed. April, 1766

FIRST DEPUTY.	SECOND DEPUTY.	WHEN ELECTED.
John Congdon,	Gideon Hoxsie,	last Tues. Aug. 1766
Peleg Cross,	" "	3d Wed. April, 1767
" "	Capt. Robert Potter,	last Tues. Aug. 1767
Capt. Robert Potter,	Joseph Stanton, Jr.,	3d Wed. April, 1768.
Joseph Stanton, Jr.,	Capt. Robert Potter,	last Tues. Aug. 1768
Gideon Hoxsie,	Job Taylor,	3d Wed. April, 1769.
" "	" "	last Tues. Aug. 1769
" "	Col. Joseph Stanton,	April 18th, 1770.
John Congdon,	Joseph Hoxsie,	August 28th, 1770.
" "	Sylvester Robinson,	April 17th, 1771.
Nathan Kenyon,	Benjamin Hoxsie, Jr.,	August 27th, 1771.
Samuel Kenyon,	" "	April 15th, 1772.
" "	Stephen Perry,	August 25th, 1772.
Sylvester Robinson,	" "	April 21st, 1773.
" "	Jonathan Hazard,	August 31st, 1773.
" "	Jesse Champlin,	April 18th, 1774.
" "	" "	August 30th, 1774.
Joseph Hoxsie,	Samuel Kenyon,	April 19th, 1775.
Capt. Jos'h Stanton, Jr.,	Jesse Champlin,	last Tues. Aug. 1775
" "	Jonathan Hazard,	April 17th, 1776.
Col. Jos'h Stanton, Jr.,	" "	last Tues. Aug. 1776
Gideon Hoxsie,	Robert Congdon,	3d Wed. April, 1777
Col. Gideon Hoxsie,	" "	last Tues. Aug. 1777
Col. Jos'h Stanton, Jr.,	Jonathan Hazard,	3d Wed. April, 1778.
Col. Gideon Hoxsie,	" "	last Tues. Aug. 1778
Col. Jos'h Stanton, Jr.,	" "	April 21st, 1779.
Brig. Jos'h Stanton, Jr.,	" "	August 31st, 1779.
Col. Gideon Hoxsie,	Brig. Jos'h Stanton, Jr.,	April 19th, 1780.
" "	" "	August 29th, 1780.
Brig. Jos'h Stanton, Jr.,	Jonathan Hazard,	April 18th, 1781.
" "	" "	last Tues. Aug. 1781
" "	Col. Gideon Hoxsie,	3d Wed. April, 1782.
" "	Jonathan Hazard,	last Tues. Aug. 1782
" "	" "	3d Wed. April, 1783.
" "	" "	August 26th, 1783.
" "	Samuel Cross,	3d Wed. April, 1784.
" "	Nathan Kenyon,	August 31st, 1784.
" "	James Congdon, Jr.,	April 20th, 1785.
" "	" "	last Tues. Aug. 1785
Thomas Hoxsie,	Jonathan J. Hazard,	April 19th, 1786.
" "	" "	August 29th, 1786.
" "	" "	3d Wed. April, 1787.

FIRST DEPUTY.	SECOND DEPUTY.	WHEN ELECTED.
Jonathan J. Hazard,	Lodowick Stanton,	August 28th, 1787.
Gen. Jos'h Stanton, Jr.,	Jonathan Hazard, Jr.,	April 16th, 1788.
" "	" "	August 26th, 1788.
" "	" "	April 15th, 1789.
Joseph Hoxsie,	Peleg Cross,	August 25th, 1789.
Gen. Jos'h Stanton, Jr.,	Jonathan Macomber,	April 21st, 1790.
Joseph Hoxsie,	James Peckham,	August 31st, 1790.
Gideon Hoxsie,	Robert Congdon,	April 20th, 1791.
Benjamin Hoxsie, Jr.,	Capt. Amos Green,	August 30th, 1791.
" "	" "	April 18th, 1792.
Peleg Cross, Jr.,	Robert Congdon,	August 28th, 1792.
" "	" "	April 17th, 1793.
Robert Congdon,	Edward Wilcox,	August 27th, 1793.
" "	" "	April 16th, 1794.
Edward Wilcox,	Gen. Jos'h Stanton,Jr.,	August 26th, 1794.
Gen. Joseph Stanton,	Edward Wilcox,	April 15th, 1795.
" "	" "	August 25th, 1795.
" "	" "	April 20th, 1796.
" "	Major Edward Wilcox,	August 30th, 1796.

In the Schedule of June, 1797, the title of "Deputies" was changed to "Representatives."

FIRST REPRESENTATIVE.	SECOND REPRESENTATIVE.	WHEN ELECTED.
Gen. Joseph Stanton,	Major Edward Wilcox,	April 19th, 1797.
" "	Col. Gideon Hoxsie,	August 29th, 1797.
" "	" "	April 18th, 1798.
" "	" "	August 28th, 1798.
" "	Capt. Jos'h Hoxsie, Jr.,	3d Wed. April, 1799.
Peleg Cross, Jr.,	Major Edward Wilcox,	August 27th, 1799.
" "	" "	April 16th, 1800.
" "	" "	August 26th, 1800.
Maj. Edward Wilcox,	Joseph Stanton, 3d,	April 15th, 1801.
" "	Joseph Stanton, Jr.,	August 25th, 1801.
" "	" "	April 21st, 1802.
" "	" "	August 31st, 1802.
" "	" "	April 20th, 1803.
" "	" "	August 30th, 1803.
" "	" "	April 18th, 1804.
" "	" "	August 28th, 1804.
" "	" "	April 17th, 1805.
" "	" "	August 27th, 1805.
" "	" "	April 16th, 1806.

FIRST REPRESENTATIVE.	SECOND REPRESENTATIVE.	WHEN ELECTED.
Col. Edward Wilcox,	Joseph Stanton, Jr.,	August 26th, 1806.
" "	" "	April 15th, 1807.
" "	" "	August 25th, 1807.
" "	" "	April 20th, 1808.
" "	" "	August 30th, 1808.
" "	" "	April 19th, 1809.
" "	Gen. Jos'h Stanton, Jr.,	August 29th, 1809.
" "	Dea. Daniel Stanton,	April 18th, 1810.
" "	" "	August 28th, 1810.
" "	" "	April 17th, 1811.
" "	Gen. Jos'h Stanton, Jr.,	August 27th, 1811.
" "	Joseph Cross,	April 15th, 1812.
Joseph Stanton, Jr.,	Asa Church,	August 25th, 1812.
" "	" "	April 21st, 1813.
" "	" "	August 31st, 1813.
" "	" "	April 20th, 1814.
" "	" "	August 30th, 1814.
" "	" "	April 19th, 1815.
" "	" "	August 29th, 1815.
" "	" "	April 17th, 1816.
Col. Edward Wilcox,	Joseph Cross,	August 27th, 1816.
Joseph Cross,	Peleg S. Thompson,	April 16th, 1817.
" "	" "	August 26th, 1817.
" "	" "	April 15th, 1818.
" "	Joseph Gavitt,	August 25th, 1818.
Joseph Gavitt,	Jesse Babcock, Jr.,	April 21st, 1819.
" "	" "	August 31st, 1819.
" "	Joseph Wilcox,	April 19th, 1820.
" "	Samuel Stanton,	August 29th, 1820.
Major Edward Wilcox,	" "	April 15th, 1821.
" "	" "	August 28th, 1821.
" "	" "	April 17th, 1822.
Thomas Hoxsie,	Arnold Hoxsie,	August 27th, 1822.
" "	George Thurston,	April 16th, 1823.
Joseph Wilcox, Jr.,	David Clark,	August 26th, 1823.
" "	" "	April 21st, 1824.
" "	" "	August 31st, 1824.
" "	" "	April 20th, 1825.
" "	" "	August 30th, 1825.
" "	" "	April 19th, 1826.
" "	" "	August 29th, 1826.
" "	Thomas Hoxsie,	April 18th, 1827.

FIRST REPRESENTATIVE.	SECOND REPRESENTATIVE.	WHEN ELECTED.
Joseph Wilcox, Jr.,	Joseph Stanton, Jr.,	August 28th, 1827.
" "	David Clark,	April 16th, 1828.
" "	" "	August 26th, 1828.
" "	" "	April 15th, 1829.
Caleb Kenyon,	" "	August 25th, 1829.
" "	Dan. King,	April 21st, 1830.
" "	" "	August 31st, 1830.
" "	" "	April 20th, 1831.
" "	" "	August 30th, 1831.
" "	" "	April 18th, 1832.
Edward Wilcox,	" "	August 28th, 1832.
" "	" "	April 17th, 1833.
Dan. King,	Caleb Kenyon,	August 27th, 1833.
" "	" "	April 16th, 1834.
Samuel Perry, Jr.,	" "	August 26th, 1834.
" "	" "	April 15th, 1835.
" "	" "	August 27th, 1835.
" "	" "	April 20th, 1836.
Caleb Kenyon,	George W. Cross,	August 30th, 1836.
George W. Cross,	James N. Kenyon,	April 19th, 1837.
" "	" "	August 29th, 1837.
" "	" "	April 18th, 1838.
" "	" "	August 28th, 1838.
" "	" "	April 17th, 1839.
Joseph Gavitt,	George A. Stanton,	August 27th, 1839.
" "	" "	April 15th, 1840.
" "	Asa Church, Jr.,	August 25th, 1840.
" "	" "	April 21st, 1841.
" "	" "	August 31st, 1841.
Asa Church, Jr.,	Gordon H. Hoxsie,	April 20th, 1842.

MEMBERS OF THE GENERAL ASSEMBLY WHO HAVE SERVED UNDER THE CONSTITUTION ADOPTED IN 1843.

SENATE.

Asa Church, Jr., 1843 to 1846.
James N. Kenyon, 1846 to 1850.
Joseph H. Cross, 1850 to 1854.
James N. Kenyon, 1854 to 1855.
William Foster, 1855 to 1857.
Asa Church, Jr., 1857 to 1858.
William Foster, 1858 to 1859.

Caleb Kenyon, 1859 to 1860.
John Money, 1860 to 1861.
Elisha S. Peckham, 1861 to 1862.
George A. Stanton, 1862 to 1864.
John W. Money, 1864 to 1865.
Hazard A. Burdick, Jr., 1865 to 1866.
Stephen C. Browning, 1866 to 1871.
Beriah C. Kenyon, 1871 to 1874.
George C. James, 1874 to

HOUSE OF REPRESENTATIVES.

Gordon H. Hoxsie, 1843 to 1844.
James N. Kenyon, 1844 to 1845.
Caleb Kenyon, 1845 to 1846.
Gideon Hoxsie, 1846 to 1847.
Asa T. Hoxsie, 1847 to 1848.
Joseph Gavitt, 1848 to 1854.
Thomas A. Pierce, 1854 to 1856.
John W. Money, 1856 to 1857.
Caleb Kenyon, 1857 to 1859.
John Congdon, 1859 to 1860.
Thomas A. Pierce, 1860 to 1861.
Calvin G. Miner, 1861 to 1862.
Asa T. Hoxsie, 1862 to 1864.
Hazard A. Burdick, 2d, 1864 to 1865.
Samuel B. Hoxsie, 1865 to 1866.
Caleb Kenyon, 1866 to 1869.
Joseph D. Wilcox, 1869 to 1872.
William D. Cross, 1872 to 1873.
Joseph C. Church, 1873 to 1874.
George Burdick, 1874 to 1875.
Charles Cross, 1875 to

TOTAL POPULATION OF WASHINGTON COUNTY, OF RHODE ISLAND, FROM 1708 TO 1875.

	Settled, or Incorporated.	1708.	1730.	1748.	1755.	1774.	1776.	1782.	1790.	1800.	1810.	1820.	1830.	1840.	1850.	1860.	1865.	1870.	1875.
CHARLESTOWN	1738		1,002		1,130	1,821	1,835	1,529	2,022	1,454	1,174	1,160	1,284	923	994	981	1,134	1,119	1,054
EXETER	1743			1,174	1,404	1,864	1,982	2,058	2,495	2,476	2,256	2,581	2,383	1,776	1,634	1,741	1,498	1,462	1,355
HOPKINTON	1757					1,808	1,845	1,735	2,462	2,276	1,774	1,821	1,777	1,726	2,477	2,798	2,512	2,682	2,760
NORTH KINGSTOWN	1674		1,200	2,105	2,109	2,472	2,761	2,328	2,907	2,794	2,957	3,007	3,036	2,909	2,971	3,104	3,166	3,668	3,505
SOUTH KINGSTOWN	1723		1,523	1,978	1,913	2,835	2,779	2,675	4,131	3,438	3,560	3,723	3,663	3,717	3,807	4,717	4,513	4,403	4,240
RICHMOND	1747			508	829	1,257	1,204	1,094	1,760	1,368	1,330	1,423	1,363	1,361	1,784	1,964	1,830	2,064	1,739
WESTERLY	1669		570	1,809	2,291	1,812	1,824	1,720	2,298	2,329	1,911	1,972	1,915	1,912	2,763	3,470	3,815	4,709	5,408
WASHINGTON COUNTY	*1729	1,770	5,554	8,406	9,676	13,869	14,230	13,133	18,075	16,135	14,962	15,687	15,421	14,324	16,430	18,715	18,468	20,697	20,061

In 1730, Westerly embraced in its territory, Charlestown, Richmond and Hopkinton. A census taken by order of the King during the same year, gave Westerly the following population, viz: Whites, 1,620; Negroes, 56; Indians, 250. Charlestown, in 1748, had the following population, viz: Whites, 641; Negroes, 58; Indians, 303. In 1875, Charlestown had a population of 1,054. Of this number, 120 persons were members of the Narragansett Tribe, and 8 non-residents, or persons of color who did not belong to the Tribe.

* Washington County was originally called the "Narragansett country." Incorporated, June 16th, 1729, as King's County, with three towns, and same territory as at the present time. Name changed to Washington County, October 29th, 1781.

CHURCHES.

The first church established in this town received the following title: "The Church of England in Charlestown." It was also called the "Westerly Church." This church was built on a lot of land given for that purpose by George Ninigret, Chief Sachem of the Narragansett Indians. It joined the Champlin farm, and when the church went down, was held by them by possession. The town of Westerly was divided after the erection of the church, and it fell on the Charlestown side of the division line. The church was situated on the north lot of the late Champlin farm, now owned by Robert Hazard, son of Joseph, and fronting on the public road, to the north of the house now owned by James McDonald, and within half a mile of the residence of the then sachem. The deed was as follows:

To all People to whom these Presents shall come, greeting.

Know ye, that I, George Ninigret, Chief Sachem and Prince of the Narragansett Indians, in the Colony of Rhode Island and Providence Plantations, in New England, in America, for and in consideration of the love and affection which I have and bear for and towards the people of the Church of England in Charlestown and Westerly, in the county of King's county, in the colony aforesaid, and for securing and settling the services and worship of God amongst them, according to the usages of that most excellent church, within the said Charlestown, at all times forever hereafter, and also for and in consideration of the sum of Five Shillings of the currency of said colony, and of the old tenor, to me in hand actually paid by John Hill, Esq., Col. Christopher Champlin, both of said Charlestown and colony aforesaid, and Ebenezer Punderson, of Groton, in the county of New London and colony, now officiates a missionary from the Society, and I was the first Episcopal of Connecticut, clerk, the receipt whereof I do hereby acknowledge, have given, granted, bargained, sold, enfeoffed, conveyed, and by these presents do fully and absolutely give, grant, bargain, sell, enfeoff, and convey, unto the said John Hill, Christopher Champlin, and Ebenezer Punderson, their heirs and assigns forever, to the use of the Society for the Propagation of the Gospel in Foreign Parts, and their successors forevermore, (which Society were incorporated by Letters Patent under the great seal of England,) one certain tract of land lying in said Charlestown, in the colony of Rhode Island aforesaid, containing forty acres, and whereon the Church of England in said Charlestown now stands, in the occupation of the aforesaid Christopher Champlin, and is butted and bounded as followeth: Beginning at a stake with stones about it, thence running south 38 degrees east 45 rods and a quarter, to a stone and heap of stones by the country road; and from thence easterly, as the road runs, 128 rods, to a stake with stones about it; from thence north 14 degrees west 40 rods to a small white oak tree marked on two sides; from thence south 50 degrees west 12 rods to a stake and stones; and from thence a straight line to the first mentioned corner; with all erections and buildings standing on said premises, with all the woods, underwoods, pools, water and water-courses, with every other appurtenance and privilege of any sort belonging to the said tract of land, or in anywise appertaining, and the reversion or reversions, and the remainders, rents, issues and profits of all and singular the premises.

To have and to hold, all and singular, the said tract of land, premises, with every of their privileges, commodities and appurtenances, unto the said John Hill, Christopher Champlin, and Ebenezer Punderson, their heirs and assigns forever, to the use and benefit and behoof of the Society for the Propagation of the Gospel in Foreign Parts, and their successors forevermore, to be by the said Society forever thereafter applied and appropriated for the benefit of the Episcopal minister for the time being of the Episcopal church in said Charlestown, in the said county of King's county, and his successors forever, and to and for no other use, intent or purpose whatsover.

And I, the said George Ninigret, do hereby, for myself, my heirs, executors, administrators, and successors in said Sachemship and Principality, and every of them, covenant and warrant to and with the said John Hill, Christopher Champlin, and Ebenezer Punderson, their heirs and assigns, and also to and with the said Society for the Propagation of the Gospel in Foreign Parts, and their successors, that I am at this present time, and by right of indefeasable inheritance, the true, lawful and absolute owner and proprietor of said premises, and the same are now free and clear of all manner of incumbrances whatever, and that I, my heirs, executors, administrators or successors, now do and forever shall and will defend all and singular the said premises, with their appurtenances, unto and to the use of them for the purpose aforesaid, against all claims and demands whatsoever. In witness whereof, I have hereunto set my hand and seal, this 14th day of January, in the year 1745 old style, or 1746 new style.　　　GEORGE —C NINIGRET.
　　　　　　　　　　　　　　　　　mark.

Acknowledged the same day, and duly recorded in the Town Clerk's Office.

THE NARRAGANSETT INDIAN CHURCH.

Many attempts were made, at different times, for the conversion of the Indians; but the missionaries were generally unsuccessful.

"About 1741, in the New Light stir, a reformation was brought about among the Indians in Charlestown, (probably under the care of a Mr. Park,) and a Baptist church soon after formed. In 1750, a Baptist church arose out of this. The first pastor was James Simons, and after him the famous Samuel Niles, in his day one of the most eminent Indian preachers in America. Others succeeded him. Benedict visited them in 1812, and found a few of the female members of the church still living and active in religious affairs; three of them about 70 years of age. The male members were all absent on a fishing voyage."

According to the most reliable information that can be educed, the old Indian church was erected somewhere about one hundred and ten years before the erection of the present one, which took place sixteen years ago; hence the old structure was built not far from 1750, and located at a little distance to the north of the center of the town, within half a mile of the Indian school-house and pond, and on the same site upon which the new edifice now stands. It was a wooden structure, built without any regard to beauty, warmth, or convenience, and quite inferior to the present church; yet there have been very many good sermons proclaimed within its walls. Here the renowned Samuel Niles poured out the gospel tidings, with amazing eloquence, to the sin-laden sons of the forest.

The new stone edifice was erected in 1859; it is twenty-eight feet wide, forty feet long, and twelve feet high, with ample room for all ordinary purposes. At the present period of time, the church contains forty members, who are Adventists in their persuasion. For a long time, the Tribe have continued to hold their annual "Indian Meetings" here, which occur on the second Sunday in August. They congregate, on this occasion, from the eastern part of Connecticut and Long Island, and from all parts of this State, to participate in these meetings and festivities. The white people, as well as the colored population, collect here in large numbers, and some of them for the express purpose of selling provisions and beer to the hungry and thirsty multitude that attend these annual gatherings. Twenty-five years ago, it was the practice of the people to meet near the church; but the great concourse of people, and the proximity of the tents, seriously affected the meetings; and since then, the Indian Council have decided that all tents shall be erected at least one mile from the meeting-house.

THE SECOND BAPTIST CHURCH OF RICHMOND.

It appears on record, that this church was founded in 1774. The old structure, which was known for a long time as the Boss Meeting-house—alas, not a stick is left to mark the once memorable spot!— was situated on the northern limit of the hill skirting the southern edge of the Richmond-town Plain, and on the west side of the road, between Clark's Mills and Usquepaug village, and between Beaver and Usquepaug rivers, on what was commonly called the Robert Stanton purchase. But on the 8th of October, 1855, the Society, which was made the recipient of a fine building lot, through the generosity of Joseph Hoxsie, Esq., erected a house of worship on the aforesaid lot, and dedicated it. The new edifice is located in Charlestown, at a little distance to the south-east of Clark's village, on the corner where the highway crosses the Shore Line Railroad, and about midway between Shannock Mills and Kenyon's Mills. In 1873, William Marchant was Clerk of the church, which then numbered seventy-nine members.

FIRST FREEWILL BAPTIST CHURCH OF RICHMOND AND CHARLESTOWN.

On the 29th of September, 1845, Rowland G. Hazard, Esq., deeded a piece of land, situated between Carolina village and the depot, at nearly equal distance, to the above-named Society. The Association erected an edifice, which was dedicated and used by the people for nearly twenty years; but, finally, on the 27th of June, 1865, Hazard G. Kenyon and wife, and William C. Tucker and wife, transferred their right, title and interest in a lot of land in the village of Carolina Mills, to the "Rhode Island Association of Freewill Baptist Churches." Here a stone basement was constructed, and the church was moved down into the village, and placed upon the foundation, by Jesse Breed, of Westerly. After the removal, the edifice underwent a thorough renovation, and it is now an ornament and a benefit to the village. The organization of this church was perfected on the 3d of August, 1866. Leander W. Tucker is the present Clerk, and his minutes indicate a membership of thirty-nine persons.

CHARLESTOWN BRANCH OF THE GENERAL SIX PRINCIPLE BAPTIST CHURCH OF RICHMOND.

The General Six Principle Baptist Church of Richmond was instituted in 1725. Rev. Gilbert Tillinghast officiates as its present pastor. In 1875, the Annual Report of the Association admitted a membership of four hundred and forty-eight persons. From this church originated the Charlestown Branch. The land on which the Charlestown Church stands was formerly owned by Ira Kenyon, Esq., who gave a deed of the same to John S. Hiscox, Trustee to the Society, June 24th, 1867. This edifice was erected at a cost of $1,500; it is twenty-eight feet wide and thirty-six feet long, and pleasantly located on high land overlooking the village of Burdick-ville and the surrounding vicinity. The church was consecrated to a divine Being, by religious ceremonies, on the 12th of January, 1871. Rev. Gilbert Tillinghast has been its regular Pastor, and Ira Kenyon, Esq., its faithful Clerk. In 1876, Mr. Kenyon's records contained the names of seventy active members. Mrs. Elizabeth Allen was admitted to a membership in the old church of Richmond in 1828; and has been a member of the new church since its organization.

FIRST BAPTIST CHURCH OF CHARLESTOWN.

Mr. Peleg Clark, Jr., of Westerly, was employed to build the church, which he completed to the satisfaction of his employers, in 1840. It is situated on the Post Road, in the vicinity of Quono-contaug Neck, and on a very pleasant elevation, commanding an extensive view of the ocean and surrounding country. The dedicatory exercises were consummated on the 11th of February, 1841. Rev. John H. Baker officiated at the dedication; and, on the next day, Feb. 12th, Wilson Cogswell was ordained a minister of the gospel, and installed the first pastor of the church. Joseph Brown succeeded Mr. Cogswell as a shepherd of the flock. In 1841, this church registered forty-three members, with Joseph W. Taylor clerk; and in 1873, seventy-one members, with Samuel B. Hoxsie clerk.

THE FIRST BAPTIST CHURCH AND SOCIETY AT CROSS' MILLS.

A deed was given by Joseph H. and George W. Cross to George Burdick, Esq., who was authorized to procure a situation for a building; and he transferred it to the Society on the 17th of June, 1876. The church, however, was built in the summer of 1873, at a cost of some $1,500, previous to the transfer of the property by Mr. Burdick. Soon after its completion, and at the organization of the church, Levi J. Cornell was chosen clerk, whose records indicate a membership of forty-three persons.

NARRAGANSETT INDIAN SCHOOL.

It appears on record, that the State began to have schools for the Narragansett Indians as early as 1765. Mr. Bennett was sent to them as teacher. The Sachem, Thomas Ninegret, petitioned "The Society to Propagate the Gospel," to establish a free school. In his letter, he closes in the following touching words :

"The prayer, that when time shall be with us no more, that when we and the children over whom you have been such benefactors shall leave the sun and stars, we shall rejoice in a far superior light."

In October, 1767, the General Assembly took into consideration a letter presented by Andrew Oliver, Esq., and voted that Thomas Ninegret and five of his council make and give to the Secretary of the Colony, a deed of an island in a certain swamp in Charlestown, containing about three acres, where stands a school-house for the use of the Indians. This agrees with what was called the old Indian school-house.

As early as 1815, the old school building was superseded by the present one, and named the Narragansett Indian School-house, in honor of the famous tribe of Indians, whose descendants still hold a small portion of the land by reservation. It may seem strange that the Indians owned the first school-house ; but it is nevertheless true. This structure stands on a small knoll, at the north end of a pond formerly known to the tribe as Quacumpaug Pond, but more recently named the School-house Pond. It is an old wooden building, having the following dimensions : Length, thirty feet ; width, twenty-four feet ; and hight, seven feet between floors. There is a rough stone chimney in the building, which gives it an ancient appearance. In this house the few surviving members of the Narragansett Indians hold their annual council, and it is here that they also have their school. Once was the time when this building occupied a central position in the community ; but time has wrought a change ; some of the tenants of the land have passed away, while others have moved to the northern and central sections of the township ; leaving the structure far away from the larger number of its patrons. The building should be condemned at once. Necessity demands an immediate and a united action on the part of the tribe to secure better facilities for the instruction of their children. It is a cold, cheerless, dilapidated institution, and the surroundings, both in and out of the building, present any thing but a favorable impression.

THE OLD SCHOOL BUILDING.

Tradition informs us that there was a school building erected in the eastern part of the town, now known as District No. 1, as early as 1775, or before the Declaration of Independence. The probability is, that this building was used for school purposes during a period of twenty years or more; however, Gen. Joseph Stanton received it by lottery, about the year 1796, and converted it into a dwelling house. One hundred years ago, the seaboard contained by far the larger portion of the town's population and opulence. Here, too, lived the better educated class of citizens; and is it to be considered strange, that such enlightened people should have fostered and encouraged the advancement of education, or should have perpetuated, in a certain sense, the institution which gave them such pre eminence and advantage? That education was deemed a great incentive and an indispensable requisite to future success, seems evident from their daily transactions of life. In the exigencies of the last century, the inhabitants of this locality founded three school buildings in succession, varying in the duration of time.

THOMAS PERRY'S SCHOOL BUILDING.

Since my first examination and research of the records of the town, I have very fortunately found a statement of a school-house that was built by Thomas Perry, at Cross' Mills, in 1801. This structure was located on the south side of the Cedar Swamp, and between forty and fifty rods to the east of the residence of George H. Ward. A school was maintained in said house for a period of more than twenty five years; but, finally, it was purchased by Doct. Dan King, who moved it up west about one mile and a half, to what was called "King's Factory," and changed it into a dwelling house. Of the information relative to said house, we have conclusive evidence; and that, from 1801 to 1828, it was the only school-house owned and used by the white people of Charlestown.

Before the school law of 1828 went into effect, the representatives of the several towns of the State were requested to furnish an exact account of the number of school-houses and schools in each town. In their report, we find one school-house, and from five to seven schools in the winter and two or three in the summer. Such substantiates the fact that the majority of schools was then kept in private residences.

FACILITIES BEFORE PUBLIC SCHOOLS.

Educational facilities prior to the establishment of public schools were exceedingly feeble in this vicinity. The people supported what were then recognized as private schools, the majority of them being kept in dwelling houses. In selecting a situation for a school, it was expedient for them to obtain a central location in the neighborhood, but this was not always accomplished, as there were very many obstacles in the way. Teachers, at this time, were hired for stipulated sums, receiving their wages from parents and guardians, who paid them in proportion to the number of pupils that each one sent to school. In this community, forty years ago, the practice was as common for a school officer to go into Connecticut to hire a teacher as it is now customary for a person to pay taxes. The school committee often granted certificates to persons whose qualifications and abilities to instruct and govern a school were quite inadequate for the task; and they seldom visited the schools to ascertain the results. Consequently, the schools were taught, many times, by very incompetent teachers; by those who could not perform all the examples in the arithmetic, and, what is much more discreditable, were unable to give satisfactory explanations of such as they could perform. It frequently happened that persons taught school who had no knowledge of grammar, or, in other words, had never studied it. The average length of schools was between three and four months; for which reason, educational resources were quite limited.

DISTRICT SYSTEM.

In 1828, the General Assembly passed an act to divide the several towns into districts, with which the people readily complied. The district system in this town was established June 2d, 1828; and a subdivision was made November 19th of the same year, separating the town into six districts. Next year, on the 15th of April, a portion of the district at Cross' Mills and at Quonocontaug was set off, forming a new district, which was added to the catalogue as No. 7. The last district subdivision in Charlestown was made in 1871, when Carolina was taken from Pasquesett, and organized as the eighth school district. In the mean time, perplexities frequently grew out of the imperfect divisions and records of the districts; and, in 1874, the school committee re-bounded all the districts, giving more definite boundaries to them, and caused the same to be placed on record in the Town Clerk's office.

DISTRICT No. 6—WASHINGTON.

In 1828, Joshua Card, Joseph Cross, Henry Greene, David Clark, Elisha Greenman, Wm. Card, Dan King, Jacob Perry, and others, agreed to build a school house. Henry Greene furnished the land, containing twenty-two square rods ; and Elisha Greenman was appointed to superintend the work. According to date, this was the first school building erected by the white people of Charlestown, which continued to be used for school purposes ; and it was named Washington, in honor of the first President of the United States. This district is situated in the northeastern part of the town. In 1871, Jason P. Greene, George W. Cross, Amos P. Greene, and Henry S. Greene, transferred the property to the district, with the proviso that when it should cease to be used for educational means, it should fall back to its original grantors ; and, in the same year, the house was thoroughly repaired, and supplied with modern desks and seats.

DISTRICT No. 4—SHUMUNCANUC.

Here, in the northwestern part of the town, the surface is very hilly, and the people named the district after the most important hill. The citizens of this section met pursuant to notice, on the premises of Abram Allen, Esq., and selected a pleasant location for a school. Mr. Allen gave, then and there, the land on which the building was to be erected ; and Mrs. Elizabeth Allen, wife of Abram, named it "Union Hill," and paid one dollar for the honor of naming it. This building was raised on the 16th of September, and dedicated, by having a meeting in it, on the 13th of November, 1834. The first structure, however, was burned down, and on November the 10th, 1845, Arnold and Nancy Hiscox deeded a parcel of land to the district, nearer the centre, whereon the present school-house stands.

Mrs. Elizabeth Allen, who was born June 22d, 1772, is now living and enjoying good health ; she is a member of the Six Principle Baptist Church of Charlestown, and possesses a remarkable memory for a person who has lived to see more than five-score years.

DISTRICT No. 2—QUONOCONTAUG.

In this section of the State, some of the hills, streams, rivers and ponds, retain at the present time the original names given by the Indians. Quonocontaug is situated in the southwestern portion of the town, and this name appears first applied to a pond in the neighborhood, from which the district received it. Edward Wilcox, who was Lieutenant Governor from 1817 to 1821, transferred a lot of land to the district, upon which a school house was built in 1838. Although a respectable number of teachers have gone forth from other schools, still this school is entitled to the honor of educating an unusual number of good and faithful teachers.

DISTRICT NO. 3—COOKSTOWN.

This division joins the town of Westerly, and it is really a rural district. The first school officers elected were the following: Bowen Briggs, Moderator; Joseph W. Taylor, Clerk; Benj. F. Wilcox, Matthias Crandall, and Rowland Peckham, Trustees; Perry Healy, Treasurer: and Gardner Crumb, Collector. Bowen Briggs and Gilbert Stanton conveyed a piece of land to the district in 1839, and a school building was erected during the year.

DISTRICT NO. 7—WATCHAUG.

The people of this district erected a school house in 1840, but a deed of the land on which the house stands was not granted until August 15th, 1864. Watchaug is located in the south part of the town, and derives its name from a large pond on the western boundary, so called by the Indians. There is no other district in Charlestown which has such a grand expanse of water within its limits, or bordering on its territory.

DISTRICT NO. 1—CROSS' MILLS.

This district is situated in the southeastern section of the town, and named after the village within its limits. The citizens of the neighborhood built a house for educational purposes in 1843. From 1845 to 1860, perhaps no school in the town excelled this one in literary attainments; and in reference to teachers, without doubt this school has produced nearly as many as all the other schools combined. The school building was repaired and re-seated in 1874.

DISTRICT NO. 5—PASQUESETT.

The citizens were in meditation a long time before any conclusion was reached; and finally, in 1850, they purchased thirty rods of land of Robert Hazard, and built a school house thereon. The district, which is situated in the northern and central part of the town, takes its name from a small pond lying on its eastern border. In 1874, the school house was enlarged and thoroughly renovated, and furnished with desks and seats of the latest pattern. The extent of territory and the advancement of the school considerably exceeds that of any other in the town. The Indian school house heretofore mentioned, is located in the southern part of this division.

DISTRICT No. 8—CAROLINA.

In 1845, Rowland G. Hazard, Esq., erected a school house in Richmond, northwest of the village; and, on the 13th of May, 1871, the property, consisting of a house and lot, was sold to the district for $700. Meanwhile, the children from the northern part of the district of Pasquesett attended school here, as it was more convenient so to do, and paid their proportion of the school fund of Charlestown to the school in Richmond. But on the 27th of January, 1872, District No. 8 of Charlestown, and No. 2 of Richmond, were consolidated, and named Carolina Joint District. At this period, an addition was made to the school house, at a cost of $2,487 63, making it a very commodious and useful school building. Immediately after the completion of the house, the school was divided into a primary and a grammar department, establishing a graded school.

IMPROVEMENT AND PRESENT CONDITION.

About forty-eight years ago, the public school system was established in the State of Rhode Island. It was truly the beginning of a new era of educational improvements; and the State, like a living body which is sensitive in every member, was touched by the noble and generous act, in all its sub-divisions. Indeed, literary interests were perceptibly awakened in the minds of the people; and, from that period onward, education has been steadily advancing in the direction of both a higher and a broader culture. The establishment of the permanent school fund and public schools gave life and vitality to the cause of education, and incited the people to a more united and determined effort to give better means of instruction to the rising generation. A few soul-inspiring men, faithful servants of a worthy cause, have taken hold of this national work, and have carried it forward to its present condition. The broad foundation of our common schools is favorably fixed, and, with wise legislation and prudent management, improvements will be made as long as time and necessity demand them. The common school is the place where a child should be taught the moral as well as the literary lessons of public life, for morality and learning are indispensable to a nation's success. Charlestown has now resident teachers enough to supply all her schools, and about fifty per cent. of them have attended State Normal Schools. The average length of schools for the year is a little more than eight months, showing quite a contrast in comparison with the school year of one half century ago.

SCHOOL SUPERVISION.

The School Committee which appointed the first Town Superintendent were elected in April, 1871, and organized soon after, by electing Samuel B. Hoxsie, Chairman; Benjamin F. Greenman, Clerk; and Dr. A. A. Saunders, Superintendent. The employment of a person to thoroughly inspect the schools, and to direct and assist the teachers in their daily labors, was an important step in educational progress, School supervision is the foundation on which the whole system of popular instruction rests. Unquestionably, what is most needed by our public schools, and what is most essential to their efficiency, is a constant, thorough, and impartial supervision. I believe that the more direct and frequent this oversight is, when judiciously exerted, the more satisfactory will be the results.

DISTINGUISHED PERSONS.

In connection with the public schools, perhaps, it may be proper to mention some of the persons who have labored faithfully for the advancement of education, and those who have become distinguished for their ability. Dan King was an earnest advocate for popular education, and his sons were educated for various professions. Joshua Card was a notable aid in the cause of public instruction. He was himself a teacher of good repute, and his youngest son, David Card, is now a physician at Willimantic, Connecticut. Dr. Joseph H. Griffin was an earnest laborer for the advancement of schools and the education of his children. Louis P. Griffin, his son, completed a course of studies in medicine, and began his practice in Chicago, Illinois. Samuel J. Cross was an able and efficient educator. He moved from Rhode Island to New York, where he became connected with a college during the remainder of his life. Wm. H. Perry, a teacher of large experience, has done much to promote the best interests of our schools. Kate Stanton, daughter of George A. Stanton, and a lecturer of some note, was formerly a teacher in this town.

EVENING SCHOOLS.
DISTRICT No. 5—PASQUESETT.

The first Evening School of Charlestown was opened in 1871, by the author of this sketch, who organized and taught it without compensation. Reynolds K. Hoxsie, Esq., offered the basement of his new house at Carolina Station, for the benefit of the school, where he has since re-opened the room for the sale of dry goods and groceries. Necessity, the mother of invention, seemed to demand the organization of the school, that a certain class of individuals who were deprived of the advantages of day schools by their several occupations might be better educated. Here the school, which registered twenty-five, and averaged eighteen pupils, continued sixteen evenings, with gratifying success. Through the labors of this school, a deep impression rested on the minds of the pupils ; they were aroused to a conciousness that more thorough and extensive knowledge of the common branches was needful for the preparation of those who were to fill the various and responsible positions of life. No motive other than a generous one prompted this effort, which has proved an invaluable blessing to the pupils who attended the school, and to the surrounding community.

DISTRICT No. 5—PASQUESETT.

In the autumn of 1872, having been convinced that illiteracy existed to some extent in our midst, I called together the children of Shannock Mills and vicinity, and established an evening school. This school was located in Charlestown ; it continued ten weeks, numbered fifteen, and gave a general average of twelve pupils. I took upon myself the responsibility of furnishing room and means, without remuneration, to secure the largest attendance ; and imparted instruction to them gratuitously. However, this school numbered less than the one taught at Carolina Station the previous year ; as the former included the pupils of two villages, whereas the latter included those of only one village. I fully appreciate the motives which influence a community to make such exertion that will confer the highest educational benefit upon the largest number of persons. To advance the cause of education in this locality, seems to be the voice and inclination of the majority of the people.

CAROLINA JOINT DISTRICT.

On the 3d day of January, 1876, Abel Tanner, an earnest, able, and efficient educator, employed Wm. T. Collins of Hopkinton, and John Holden of Charlestown, as teachers. With their assistance, he established an evening school in Carolina Joint District, in the town of Richmond, which proved a real success, and met the approbation of all concerned. Idleness and stupidity were soon excluded from the premises ; the latent energies of the mind were awakened and called into action ; the enthusiasm and zeal of 1871 were rekindled ; and the school marched onward to perfection amidst the congratulations of the pupils and the approval of the people. This school held twenty-nine evening sessions, registered sixty-four, averaged fifty-eight, and closed February 24th, 1876.

During the next winter, Mr. Tanner, who was then trustee of the district, engaged Wm. T. Collins of Hopkinton, E. Anson Stillman of Westerly, and Wm. F. Tucker of Charlestown, and again opened the school, which continued only eighteen evenings, registered fifty-nine, and averaged forty-nine. The teachers worked earnestly and conscientiously for the advancement of those under their superintendence, while the pupils manifested an anxious desire to learn, and make the most of their opportunities. The best of discipline was maintained throughout the term, and the average attendance, for an evening school, was very good. The urgent need of maintaining an evening school of this grade and character, in this thriving village of some five hundred inhabitants, is obvious to any rational mind. It is my earnest desire that the success which the school has gained during the two past terms, and the interest and zeal manifested by the pupils for whose benefit it is organized, will secure its continuation. Term began December 12th, 1876, and ended February 13th, 1877.

DISTRICT No. 4—SHUMUNCANUC.

The first evening school in this district was opened December 15th, 1876, and closed March 3d, 1877. Mr. Simon P. Nichols, of Usquepaugh, who was teacher in the day school, took charge of it, and performed his duties with marked success and ability. Owing to the small number of pupils in attendance, and the larger part of that number being members of the day school, the principal difficulty of the instructor was to awaken earnestness and enthusiasm in the minds of the pupils. Notwithstanding the many disadvantages under which the teacher has been obliged to labor, yet the time has not been wholly lost, nor the means entirely squandered. The entire number registered was sixteen, and the average attendance for the term was nine. The school closed its session of twenty-five evenings, of three hours each, with a public exhibition.

DISTRICT No. 5—PASQUESETT.

In the latter part of September, 1876, the citizens and friends of education persuaded me to establish an evening school where it would accommodate to the best advantage the scholars of Shannock, Clark, and Kenyon's villages. My first business was to procure a suitable room in a central position. This desired situation I found in the possession of Simeon P. Clark, of whom I hired it, and fitted it up for the occasion. Clark's Hall is well known to the public; it

is the largest one in Charlestown ; and it is generally used for religious meetings and educational gatherings. To select a compe-
tent corps of teachers was the next task that devolved upon me,
and I very readily made a choice of Abel Tanner, Wm. T. Collins,
and John Holden. The school became organized on the 16th day
of October, 1876, and everything progressed finely and favorably.
The pupils were divided into the following classes: In spelling,
three classes ; in reading, four classes ; in arithmetic, four classes ;
in grammar, two classes ; in algebra, one class ; in penmanship,
one class ; and in Town's Analysis of Derivative Words, one
class. The whole number of pupils registered during the term was
75 ; the average attendance, 57 ; average age of pupils in attendance, 20 years. The school closed its term of twenty-six evenings
on the 5th day of February, 1877.

MANUFACTORIES.

Charlestown cannot be considered a manufacturing district, as
there is no capital employed in cotton or woolen manufactories
within its limits. A few manufacturers, however, reside in this
town, but their places of business are located on the right bank of
Pawcatuck River, and in the town of Richmond, where all the manufacturing establishments are situated, which furnish employment
to a portion of the inhabitants in the northern part of this town.

On the 14th of February, 1776, Charles Church was authorized
by a vote of the town to make thirty gun-barrels and bayonets for
the use of the town ; the gun barrels were to be not less than three
feet and six inches long ; and that the said Charles Church be allowed one dollar per foot for gun-barrels thus made, and one dollar
for each bayonet.

Caleb Crandall was authorized, at the same meeting, to stock in
a strong and sufficient condition, for the use of soldiers, thirty
small arms, and that the said Caleb Crandall be allowed $1 25 for
each gun stocked as aforesaid.

Joseph Stanton and Caleb Crandall were likewise appointed a
committee to make a contract with Daniel Saunders for thirty gun-
locks and trimmings, and to agree with him upon the price of them.

KNOWLES' PURCHASE.

On the 17th of March, 1845, Lodowick Hoxsie* sold to John T.

---

* Lodowick Hoxsie, Esq., who bought the saw-mill and situation of Job Card,
more than sixty years ago, or as early as 1815, ran the mill for a number of years
after he came into possession of it. The mill was built by Mr. Card, at a very early
date, but a portion of the old structure was removed since 1840.

and Jirah Knowles a mill privilege, situated on the south bank of
the river at Clark's Mills. The new firm went to work, erected a
mill, and manufactured linsey goods. Samuel A. Hoxsie bought
the property, August the 1st, 1848, converted the establishment
into a cotton mill, and made cotton yarn until 1856, when it was
burned down. The site is now in the possession of Simeon P.
Clark, who owns the land on both sides of the stream at the falls.

KING'S PURCHASE.

It is well known that Dan King bought a certain tract of
land of Joseph Stanton, March 16th, 1831, and built himself a
small mill, in which he manufactured negro cloth. "King's Factory," for so it was called, was situated on the road between Cross'
Mills and Richmond Switch, now known as Wood River Junction,
and about one and one-quarter miles west from the first-named
place. Finally, on the 22d of February, 1841, John R. Congdon
purchased the estate of Mr. King. Congdon then received John
Miller as partner in the enterprise, and changed the mill into a
twine manufacturing establishment. Here the firm pursued this
branch of business for a few years, but at last all went down, business, pond, and houses. The spindles have ceased to hum, the
wheel has surely passed away, and there is not one building left—
no, not one stick—at the present time, to remind one of the business
that was transacted here. George F. Burdick, Esq., now cultivates
the land where the pond once flowed. Of the manufacturing establishments of this town, such seems to be the destiny.

GRIST MILL.

The first information relating to a grist mill, is found on record
in Ninegret's deed to the colony, dated March 28, 1709. This mill
then belonged to Joseph Davill, and was located on the brook at
Cross' Mills, where the present one stands ; but I am unable to
find, in my researches, the exact date when the mill was first built.
This grist mill was in a good working condition when Joseph Davill
owned it ; and it has been in use up to the present time. This is
the only grist mill in the town, and Peleg Cross and his heirs have
held possession of it for a long time ; it has, however, changed
hands since the death of George W. and Joseph H. Cross, and it is
new owned by Alfred Collins and Benjamin B. Greene.

SAW MILLS.

About 1½ miles south of Carolina village, on the road leading to

Cross' Mills, and something less than one mile to the north-east of the Indian cedar swamp, is a saw mill, which was owned by Joseph Jeffrey about one hundred years ago, and then known as the old Indian saw mill. The precise date of this mill is not known, it may have been built as early as Joseph Davill's mill, which was in good running order in 1709. Joseph Jeffrey sold this property to Caleb Kenyon, from whom it was handed down to his posterity. In 1864, Saunders Crandall purchased the estate of Caleb Kenyon's heirs ; and, after the lapse of two or three years, he sold the farm to Benjamin F. Crandall, and the mill and privilege to Benjamin Tucker, who rebuilt and enlarged the mill, making several improvements. The building now contains a saw mill and a shingle mill, which are in operation during the larger part of the year. When Mr. Kenyon came into possession of this mill, the forests and swamps contained excellent timber. Oak, pine and cedar, are the principal kinds of lumber sawed at this establishment.

Tradition informs us that Joseph Jeffrey was a wheelwright as well as a sawyer by trade ; and the people wishing to gain some knowledge of his workmanship, asked him to tell them how he succeeded in making such splendid wheels ; whereupon he replied, " I guess and 'low, and the work generally comes all right."

TUCKER'S SHINGLE MILL.

In 1833, John Tucker, then a young man, built a dam, raised a pond, and erected a shingle mill. In three or four years after this, the Providence and Stonington railroad passed through the northern part of the town, within ten or fifteen rods of the mill. Carolina Depot, the nearest station to the establishment, is situated about one half of a mile to the east of it. Mr. Tucker informed me that since he commenced operations in 1833, his mill has turned out more than two hundred thousand shingles annually, or nearly ten millions. Possibly this mill has sawed, in forty-three years, more shingles than any other establishment in Washington County.

INDIAN BURYING GROUND.

About one mile to the north-east of Cross' Mills, and nearly the same distance to the north of the late Gen. Joseph Stanton's residence, now owned by Doct. John A. Wilcox, is located the ancient burial-place of the royal family of the Narragansett Indians. It is on a pleasant elevation, which commands an extensive view of the ocean and country. There is a little pond to the south of it, and perhaps within eighty rods of the famous burying ground. There is one row of mounds raised above the next, where Indian tradition identifies them as the tombs of the sachems, great men, and their families. Many of the graves are very lengthy. The hill was formerly covered with wood, but during the great gale of the 8th of September, 1869, some of it was prostrated, and since then Joseph H. and George W. Cross, proprietors of the land, (now deceased,) have cut off a portion of the timber. This property, however, was recently sold at auction, to Edward T. Burdick and Benjamin B. Greene.

In May, 1859, an event of a peculiar nature, which has a direct bearing upon this subject, transpired in this town, and it may with propriety be mentioned here. The following citizens—Joshua P. Card, Charles Cross, George F. Babcock, John Congdon, Asa Noyes, Christopher P. Card, Oliver Fisk, Samuel Noca, and Benoni Henry —who formed a company of nine members, repaired to the noted " Indian Burying Hill," and there opened a grave, to ascertain in what manner the Indians buried their dead, and to obtain, or collect, if possible, a few of the relics said to be deposited in the graves, as it was customary for them so to do. The grave which they opened was covered with large flat stones, and contained a log coffin. Two logs were split open, making four pieces; these pieces served as bottom, sides and top of the coffin; and were firmly bound together with iron chains. A brass kettle was found at one end of the coffin, and an iron kettle at the other end. Quite a large collection of relics were taken out of this grave, and carried to the village at Cross' Mills, whence a portion of them were sent to Brown University in Providence, as I have been informed.

A suit was brought against these men, by Henry Hazard, Joshua Noca, and Gideon Ammons, of the tribe, for opening the grave and taking therefrom sundry articles, or, in other words, for crime and misdemeanor against the laws of the State of Rhode Island. They were arraigned before Joseph H. Griffin, Justice of the Peace, examined, and held to answer therefor before the Supreme Court at Kingston, where they were duly acquitted, and exonerated from blame. The justice court over which Mr. Griffin presided was held in the Ocean House at Cross' Mills, for the special occasion.

Subsequently, Dr. Parson, of Providence, opened quite a number of graves, to obtain a supply for a repository of scientific curiosities. Those who saw his collection make the assertion, that he did not accumulate one half as many relics as the party found in the first grave, against whom the prosecution was directed.

There is another Indian burying ground on Fort Neck, near the site of the old fort, where several graves are now visible. On one of the grave stones, (and the only one on which there seems to be any letters,) is the following inscription: "Here lies the Body of George, the son of Charles Ninegret, King of the Natives, and of Hannah his wife, died December the 22d, 1732, aged 6 mo."

CHARLESTOWN LIBRARY ASSOCIATION.

At a meeting of the subscribers for a Library to be established in the town of Charlestown, held pursuant to notice given by a number of said subscribers, at the house of James Fry in said town, January 17th, A. D. 1849, John Stanton, Esq., was appointed Chairman of said meeting, and Wm. H. Perry, Secretary. The meeting proceeded to appoint a Committee to draft a Constitution ; the following persons were appointed the Committee: Dr. Joseph H. Griffin, Wm. H. Perry, George W. Cross, Asa Church, and John Stanton. On motion, the meeting was adjourned to Wednesday, January 24th, 1849, at 6½ o'clock P. M., to meet at this place.

WM. H. PERRY, *Sec'y.*

At a meeting of the subscribers for a Library to be established in the town of Charlestown, held by adjournment at the house of James Fry in said town, Wednesday, January 24th, 1849, John Stanton, Esq., in the chair. The Committee appointed to draft a Constitution made report, presenting a draft of Constitution, and the same being read, was taken up by sections and acted upon, and finally the whole embodiment was adopted as the Constitution. John Stanton, Esq., was elected President ; George W. Cross, Vice President ; and Dr. Joseph H. Griffin, Secretary, of the Association. Dr. Joseph H. Griffin was appointed first Librarian, Samuel B. Hoxsie second, and Charles Anthony third Librarian. Wm. H. Perry was appointed Treasurer. A code of By-Laws was presented, taken up by sections and acted upon, and adopted as the By-Laws of the Association. On motion being made, the meeting was adjourned *sine die.* JOSEPH H. GRIFFIN, *Sec'y.*

CONSTITUTION.

We, the subscribers, agree to associate and incorporate ourselves for the purpose of establishing and maintaining a Public Library in the town of Charlestown, under the provisions of an act entitled "An act to provide for the voluntary incorporation of Library, Academy and School Associations," passed at the June session of the General Assembly, A. D. 1847 ; and to be governed by the following Constitution :

ART. 1. This Association shall be called the Charlestown Library Association.

ART. 2. The officers of the Association shall be a President, Vice-President, Secretary, Treasurer, and three Librarians, and the three first-named officers shall constitute a Board of Directors, who shall manage the business of the Association, subject, however, to such rules and regulations as the Association may from time to time adopt. A majority of the persons elected Directors shall be a quorum, and they shall meet from time to time, whenever notified by the President. Either of the two last-named offices, (i. e., Treasurer or Librarian,) may be held by either of the three first-named officers. The officers of this Association shall serve without pecuniary emolument.

ART. 3. The annual meeting shall be held on the fourth Wednesday of January in each year. All the officers of this Association shall be elected by ballot, if demanded by any five members, at the annual meeting thereof; *provided*, however, that the first election of officers shall take place at the time of the adoption of this Constitution. The Treasurer shall be required to give bond to the Association for the faithful discharge of his duties.

ART. 4. Any member, for disorderly or immoral conduct, or for refusing or neglecting to comply with the By-Laws of the Association, may be expelled, and any officer, for misconduct, may be removed, at any regularly notified meeting of said Association.

ART. 5. The Directors may make all such regulations as they think best for the government of the Library, and calculated to enlarge the benefits thereof ; *provided*, they be not inconsistent with law, or the Constitution, or the By-Laws of the Association.

ART. 6. The Library shall be held by the Association, not in shares for the benefit of the shareholders, but in trust for the benefit of the public ; to be open to all who shall comply with the regulations made by the Association or Directors. And for the purpose of continuing the legal existence of the corporation, the Association shall, from time to time, elect as members such persons as they shall think most likely to co-operate zealously in promoting its objects. But no person shall be elected or admitted as a member unless proposed at a previous meeting ; *provided*, however, that all persons who shall have subscribed the sum of one dollar for the establishment of said Library before this Constitution is adopted, shall, on paying to the proper officer the amounts by them subscribed, within the time prescribed by the Association, become members of the same, without being propounded at a previous meeting, as fully and effectually as those subscribers who are admitted at the time said Constitution is adopted.

ART. 7. The President may at any time, and shall on the request of the Directors, or of any five members, call meetings of the Association, giving ten days public notice ; but the Association may, from time to time, regulate the mode of notice, and may direct when such meetings shall be held.

ART. 8. This Constitution may be amended at any annual meeting, *provided* notice of the intended amendment has been given at some previous meeting. The Secretary shall cause this Constitution, and all alterations or amendments thereof, to be recorded in the Records of Land Evidence of the town of Charlestown, as the law requires.

MEMBERS OF THE ASSOCIATION.

John Stanton,	Joseph B. Tucker,
Joseph H. Griffin,	Stephen C. Browning,
Asa Church, Jr.,	Joseph H. Cross,
George W. Cross,	James L. Austin,
Peleg T. Brightman,	John D. Browning,
Gordon H. Hoxsie,	Charles Cross,
Gilbert Taylor,	Benjamin B. Green,
Samuel B. Hoxsie,	James Fry,

J. P. Card.

Recorded January 2d, A. D. 1850, by G. Hoxsie, Jr., Town Clerk.

The Charlestown Library Association was established in 1850, and owes its origin mainly to the liberality of Amasa Manton, Esq., of Providence. By the expenditure of about one hundred and fifty dollars, he has been instrumental in raising in this town double that amount, and has thus secured the establishment of a library with five hundred good books. Since the accomplishment of this object, the citizens have added at least one hundred and fifty volumes to the catalogue, making in all about six hundred and fifty volumes. Who can estimate the innumerable blessings, individual and social, which will flow directly or indirectly from the dissemination of these books, and which will continue to flow still more abundantly when the liberal donor has himself passed from the earth, and another generation has risen up to have access to this library?

There is not one clause in the Constitution, By-Laws, Rules and Regulations of the Association, whereby it is made an itinerating library; yet the society established it, and divided the books into three divisions, locating them as follows: First division, at Cross' Mills, in charge of Dr. Joseph H. Griffin, first librarian; second division, at Quonocontaug Neck, in care of Samuel B. Hoxsie, second librarian; and the third division, at Carolina Mills, in care of Charles Anthony, third librarian. The volumes are now placed in cases, and are under the supervision of George H. Ward of Cross' Mills, Samuel B. Hoxsie of Quonocontaug, and Joseph B. Tucker of Carolina Mills.

This library, for the last ten or fifteen years, has been comparatively useless. I do earnestly hope that the friends of education will place these most powerful means of accomplishing the promotion of knowledge and virtue, upon a more sure basis, that the town may have its annual State appropriation, and that the people may avail themselves of the rare advantages which are indispensable to a well-informed community.

Abel F. Stanton, of Cross' Mills, is the present Secretary of the Association.

EDIFICES AND HALLS.

A brief history of these structures may cast a ray of light on the gradual advancement of better facilities for both public and private affairs. Larger and more commodious halls have been provided for the use of the people. Previous to 1848, this town had but one hall; since then, five more have been added to the number.

STANTON'S HALL.

As early as 1796, Gen. Joseph Stanton, through a lottery, obtained a school building, which he afterward enlarged and fitted up for a dwelling house. However, this building underwent several improvements, and about the year 1810, the house received the addition of a store and hall; and from that period onward to the time when the cars and steamboats were brought into use, it was a tavern of no small importance. Here many of the leading men of the country met, as it was on the most direct route between Newport and New London, and nearly midway between the two cities. In the noted and time-worn mansion, we find the oldest, and doubtless the first, hall ever erected in this town; but, during the last thirty years, it has ceased to be used for public convenience. The estate is now owned by John A. Wilcox, M. D., who has recently made some repairs on the buildings.

WARD'S HALL.

In 1848, the Ocean House, at Cross' Mills, contained a hall which was opened for public use. The most memorable event which transpired in this hall was the criminal prosecution brought against the party who opened the grave on "Indian Burying Hill." Peleg Sisson, Esq., in 1871, purchased this property, and divided the hall into smaller rooms; therefore, as a hall, it has passed into desuetude.

CROSS' HALL.

In 1855, Joseph H. and George W. Cross put up a stone building, 26 by 36 feet on the ground, and used the basement for a store and post-office, and the upper story for a public hall. The town meetings and town councils were convened in this hall from 1855 to 1876, or more than one quarter of a century; but the building has been vacated since the death of Joseph H. Cross, who died May 25th, 1876.

CLARK'S HALL.

In 1859, John T. Knowles erected a grain mill, 44 by 40; but, after taking another view of the situation, he finally converted the establishment into a four-family tenement-house. In 1869, Simeon P. Clark & Co. bought the estate of Samuel and Edwin Knowles, sons of John T. Knowles. During the same year, Mr. Clark employed Charles Maxson & Co. of Westerly, who changed the upper story of the building into a hall, put on a sharp roof in lieu of the flat one, supplied the hall with a belfry and bell, and made a very spacious and convenient room of it. Of the four halls in the town, this is the largest one, and the one most frequently used. The chief object for which this hall was constructed, as Mr. Clark informed me, was to afford better accommodation to the people for religious and educational purposes. How wise a devotion for the people's promotion! This chapel seems to be in the most central place ; and it is opened for religious meetings, for Sabbath-schools, for Singing-schools, for evening-schools, and for the general diffusion of knowledge.

CARD'S HALL.

Some time in the early part of 1871, Henry C. Card, of Cross' Mills, entered into a contract with Jonathan Tucker for a building having the following dimensions : Length, 36 feet ; and width, 2G feet. Mr. Tucker completed the job according to agreement during the same year. This structure consists of two departments, a grocery store and a public hall ; the latter, however, is now used by the town for public business.

SAMOSET HALL.

The structure, including the hall at Carolina Mills, was built in 1872. It is 50 feet in length by 30 feet in breadth ; and it is superior to any other edifice of the kind in Charlestown, both in design and workmanship. Soon after the completion of this building, William D. Cross, the proprietor, established a cigar manufactory on the lower floor, where he is still actively engaged in the business.

The Richmond and Charlestown Teachers' Association, which was organized in the early part of December, 1874, has always assembled in this hall, as it is near the boundary between the two towns, and affords altogether the best accommodation to the people who attend such educational meetings. May this hall be in constant demand, and the center of refinement and learning !

INDEX.

www.ingramcontent.com/pod-product-compliance
Lightning Source LLC
Chambersburg PA
CBHW020046030726
47499CB00007B/2612